Family Ties

The Lyons Garden Book One

D.M. Foley

Remember Your Roots Press

ISBN: 979-8-9876505-2-3 (Paperback Ingram)

Cover Design by: Dawns Designs

Printed in the United States of America

To my husband and my sons. Thank you for supporting me in following my dreams. I am blessed with the love of all of you. I hope I inspire you all to follow your dreams, no matter how long they take to come true.

To my mom. Thank you for encouraging my love of reading and writing. Without that encouragement, my creativity would not have blossomed.

To my dad. I hope you are watching over me from heaven and smiling down at me. You always said I could do anything I put my mind to. Well, here I go, putting my mind to writing and publishing my first book.

To my brother. Thank you for always having my back in everything I do.

To Mrs. Hans. My high school English teacher. Thank you for helping me hone my writing skills and for assigning us influential books to read. It was in your class that the character of Jessica Greenhall came to life.

To C.W. Thank you for encouraging me to follow my writing dreams. Thank you for also being a sounding board and a constructive critic.

Contents

CHAPTER ONE

Who am I?

WALKING TO THE MAILBOX, Jessica noticed the crispness of the air as the wind swirled leaves across the driveway. It always filled fall in New England with beautiful colors and scents. However, Winter, Spring, and Summer brought their own delightful bombardments to her senses, which is why she lived here in the small town of Preston, Connecticut. Nestled on fifty acres of land, the small log cabin she owned is where she lived. In the Fall, she especially enjoyed the long walk down her driveway over the little wooden bridge that spanned the babbling brook running through her property.

Grabbing her mail out of the mailbox, one piece of mail caught her attention, and she felt a tinge of excitement bubbling inside her. It was the DNA kit she had ordered off the internet through a genealogy website. *Will she finally find out who she is and where she comes from?* Her parents were very loving people whom she loved very much, and a small feeling of guilt crept into her gut. *They would understand,* she told herself.

Noreen and Glen Greenhall could not have children of their own and after years of unsuccessful fertility treatments, had adopted Jessica. The diagnosis of breast cancer in Noreen in 2008 compelled them to tell Jessica about the adoption. It had been a closed one that an attorney friend of theirs had orchestrated. All she knew of her biological mother was that she was an unwed teenage mother who gave birth to her when she was sixteen in 1992.

Being adopted wasn't much of a shock to Jessica. She had long suspected it. She looked nothing like either of her parents. Her green eyes and dazzling red hair with its long curls were such a stark contrast to her mom's blonde hair and brown eyes and her dad's brown hair and blue eyes. There was no way they were her biological parents. Her parents were also much older than her peers' parents. They had adopted her when they were in their early forties. What was shocking was how quickly Noreen's cancer had spread and how none of the treatments worked. The disease abruptly took the woman she called mom all her life from her within a year of her diagnosis.

Losing her mother left such an emptiness inside her, she couldn't even describe it. That was when she asked herself *who am I?* At first, it was a little nagging in her gut; she tried to quiet by taking nature hikes at Bluff Point, Hopeville Pond State Park, or Pachaug State Forest. Although, as her eighteenth birthday approached, she felt more and more compelled to find out the truth about her biological parents. Glen understood, and after losing his wife, Jessica was his world, his everything, and he would stop at nothing to make her happy. He reached out to his attorney friend, who handled the adoption. However, his friend's office had burnt to the ground and, along with it, the records of Jessica's adoption.

When Jessica turned eighteen, she tried using social media to find out who her biological mother was by posting her birth date and the hospital she was born in. Even though the posts went viral, shared thousands of times, she received no leads about who her parents were. It seemed as if there would never be a way for her to know who she was and where she came from. Her first semester at college kept her so busy she put her quest on the back burner.

Then, the unthinkable happened during her senior year of college. The only father she had ever known, the man who tried to give her everything she ever wanted, died in a tragic car accident. Her world came crashing down around her and as she struggled to finish college, the nagging question rose back into her gut: *who am I?*

She had inherited the log home and the acreage when her father passed away. Tucked away in her little serene part of Southeastern New England, she had thrown herself into her passion for nature photography and had made a name for herself, taking pictures for publications like National Geographic and even Time Magazine. In the three years since her father's passing, she had been to so many beautiful places in the world she had almost forgotten that she was alone. She had plenty of friends, however; she had no family ties.

Both her parents had been only children and their parents, her grandparents, had all died when she was very young from varying circumstances. This left her with no aunts or uncles, no cousins, and being adopted, no siblings. When a friend of hers mentioned the genealogy website and DNA kit and how it had helped her track down her family history, she figured it was worth the shot.

Now it was here, and she was holding it in her hands as she hastened back to her log cabin. When she got closer to the cabin, the knots in her stomach built. Her hands shook, and the questions flew through her mind. *What if I find my biological parents and what if they don't want to be found? Could I have brothers and sisters? What if I don't find my parents? Can I live with not knowing?*

As she climbed the steps to the cabin, she heard her house phone ringing. *Ugh, why now?* She only used her house phone for her photography business assignments, which meant her agent was calling her with a new assignment. She rushed through the doorway and hurried into her office, which was to the right of the foyer. Slightly out of breath, she answered the phone.

"Hello Ann, how are you?"

"Jessica, how long would it take you to get to East Hampton, New York?"

"Let's see, a half hour from here to the Long Island Ferry, then it's about a two-hour ride across, and then maybe one and a half hours to East Hampton from Orient Point."

"Can you be there by tomorrow afternoon? National Geographic is doing an article on Gardiners Island off the coast of East Hampton and they want you to take pictures for their article."

"Sure, send me the address and who I need to meet and I will be there. It isn't often I get to work so close to home. You are usually sending me halfway across the world."

"Jessica, very few people get to set foot on Gardiners Island. You should feel very privileged. It is one of the largest privately owned islands in our country and it has been in the same family for hundreds of years."

"Sounds intriguing. I can't wait to see it."

"I will send you the address and all the information via email as soon as we are off the phone. I trust you can make your travel arrangements?"

"Sounds like a plan. Of course, I can make my arrangements. Talk to you later, Ann."

"Good. Have a pleasant trip and call me when you get back."

Wow, a private island. I may have to do some research about this place. Jessica thought to herself as she fired up her laptop to retrieve the email Ann was sending her. As she typed Gardiners Island into her Google search bar, she remembered her DNA kit sitting on the little table in the foyer. Jessica quickly got up and got the kit. As she opened it, the knots started in the pit of her stomach again.

Following the directions in the kit, she opened up a new tab on her laptop and logged into the genealogy website, activating her kit by entering the kit number. She then opened the vial in the kit and filled the vial with spit. As she did so, she wondered how the paltry amount of saliva she was providing may help her find out who her biological parents were. Science truly was amazing sometimes. She added the blue solution provided, sealed the vial, shook the vial, and put it in the envelope to send back. She would place the kit in the mailbox on her way to Gardiners Island in the morning. Then she logged out of the genealogy website and closed the tab, returning to her search on the island.

In her quick search, Jessica learned Gardiners Island was the first English settlement in New York. Lion Gardiner settled it in 1638. He had bought the island from the Montauket Indians in a trade because of his support of them during the Pequot War. She also learned that Captain Kidd had buried treasure on the island in 1699, all of which the Gardiner family had to turn over during Captain Kidd's trial for charges of piracy. It was even the birthplace of Julia Gardiner who married President John Tyler and became First Lady in 1844. *Intriguing,* she thought to herself as she concluded her research and made reservations to take the 7:00 am ferry across the Long Island Sound.

Her schedule was to meet Arthur Brockton, the lawyer for the island's current owner, a descendant of Lion Gardiner, at 3 pm at a café in East Hampton. As Ann had told her, the island indeed had stayed in the family for hundreds of years. The current owner was a millionaire who owned a real estate development company in Manhattan. National Geographic had contacted the owner to do an article on the largest colony of osprey that lives on the island since it is one of the few locations in the world where the osprey build their nests on the ground because of the lack of natural predators. The owner was more than happy to oblige.

Jessica fell asleep that night thinking about all the intriguing history Gardiners Island held. She dreamt about pirates and buried treasure, Indians, and even about the President of the United States possibly being on the island. She never dreamed the course of her life was about to take an unsuspecting turn.

CHAPTER TWO

The affair

EAST HAMPTON, NEW YORK, is known for its old family wealth. Where many rich and famous people go on vacation during the summer. It was the summer of 1991 and Mira was spending the summer with her best friend Lena at her beach house in the Hamptons. The girls had met in the fall when they both started school at the prestigious all-girls. St. Catherine's Preparatory School in Thompson, CT.

Lena's family was from East Hampton and was part of the old wealth. Mira had gotten into St. Catherine's on a full academic scholarship. Her family was what they referred to as middle class, however, the girls hit it off the very first day they met in their dorm room and quickly became best friends. When Lena had asked her parents if Mira could stay with them for the summer, they were skeptical at first about whether Mira would feel comfortable and fit in with the Hampton social scene. Lena convinced them she would help Mira. It elated Mira's parents that Lena gave their daughter the opportunity to spend the summer with such successful people. Their motto was, *"Your success depends on who you know."*

Mira's father was an insurance salesman, and her mother was an aspiring artist. They weren't what you would call successful in terms of wealth, however with Mira being accepted into the prestigious St. Catherine's, they hoped that would change. Mira's father, Brad Kennedy, was already peddling life insurance to some of the more affluent parents at Mira's school, and some parents had already commissioned Kathleen Kennedy to paint their portraits. They knew their daughter aspired to go to Harvard Law School, so they hoped some connections they were making would help make that dream come true.

As the car pulled into the circular driveway of the beach house, the view took Mira's breath away. She never imagined the beach house would be so magnificent and large. The stone façade gave it an aged look with stone pillars accenting the wrap-around veranda. The car came to a stop, and the driver got out and opened the car door for the girls. Lena jumped out, pulling Mira out of the car with her.

"Thank you, James. Could you see to it our bags get brought up to our room?"

Lena called over her shoulder to the driver as she continued to pull Mira along toward the house.

"Yes, ma'am."

James replied as he gathered the girl's bags to bring into the beach house.

Lena brought Mira around to the back of the house where Mira caught the smell of the salt water blowing along the breeze. The view of the Atlantic ocean was spectacular as the house was right on the southern fork of Long Island. Lena's parents were sitting on the veranda drinking lemonade as the girls came over.

"Lena, Mira, we are so happy you are finally home!"

Rita, Lena's Mother stood up and embraced both girls.

"I hope you two girls are up to a party tonight. The Gardiners are having their annual start to the summer party on the island and they have invited us. Lena, you know how anyone who is anyone will be there. I am sure Mira would love it!"

"Yes, mother, we will be up to the party and I am sure Mira will love it!"

The girls went into the beach house and Lena showed Mira the room they would share for the summer. As they unpacked, Mira couldn't believe the absolute luck she had in meeting Lena and befriending her. The bedroom had two double beds with lilac bed shams and what seemed to be a dozen throw pillows on each. The walls were a very pale purple, and the trim was a brilliant white. It looked like the furniture was old pine.

There was a bathroom connected to their room with a claw-footed bathtub that Mira couldn't wait to take a nice soaking bath in.

"Mira, you can borrow any of my clothes in the closet over there. I have dozens of sundresses. I am sure you will find one that will be perfect for the party tonight."

Lena pointed to the walk-in closet.

"Oh my gosh, Lena! This closet is the size of my bedroom back home!"

Mira looked through Lena's extensive wardrobe.

Lena chose a pale yellow strapless sundress and paired it with white sandals. Mira chose an emerald green strapless sundress and paired it with a pair of tan sandals. The girls did their hair and makeup, copying the latest *Teen Beat* magazine styles. They painted their fingernails and toenails. Mira's heart pounded, and her stomach swirled with mixed emotions. As much as Lena treated her as her equal, she knew others in the Hampton social scene might not be as accepting. Lena looked at her friend and saw the worry on her face, the way she always furrowed her brows when she was deep in thought.

"Hey, what's got you worried?"

"This is all surreal. It's amazing, but I am concerned that people will find out I am not one of you."

"I already told you. Be mysterious. Your last name will be enough for people to accept you. They will assume you are one of us. Trust me, once they hear you're a Kennedy, they will fall all over you!"

"I am a Kennedy, but I am not one of those Kennedys."

"I know that and you know that. They don't have to know that."

"Girls! It's time to go!"

Rita called up the stairs.

They piled into the car and headed to the private ferry that would take them all over to Gardiners Island. Lena had given Mira the rundown on the Gardiners and their famous island while they were unpacking and getting ready for the party. Richard Gardiner shared ownership of the island with a cousin. Richard, twenty-four, just married another East Hampton socialite, Mary Klein.

As they pulled up to the manor house on the island, Mira saw the throngs of people milling around the outside of the house laughing and socializing. She noticed how sophisticated and glamorous they all looked. That feeling of dread crept through her. Lena squeezed her friend's hand to reassure her and as the door to the car opened for them, the feeling subsided and pure excitement took over. There was a couple welcoming everyone, and Mira automatically recognized they must be Richard and Mary. Soon it was their turn to be welcomed and as they introduced Mira to Richard, she felt like she was in a dream.

She couldn't remember what she had said when he had reacted to hearing she was a Kennedy. All she could remember was how he took her hand and ever so gently brought it to his lips while his deep, icy blue eyes pierced through her soul and lit her on fire. Mira had never felt like this before. As she walked away with Lena, she felt the yearning to turn around and gaze into those eyes again.

She resisted well, though, telling herself, *He's married, and he is nine years older than you!*

"Oh my God, Mira! Did you see how he was looking at you?"

Lena swooned as soon as they were out of earshot of her parents.

"See it? Lena. I felt his gaze piercing through me! He is the most gorgeous man I have ever seen!"

"He is married!"

"I know. Tell him that, though!"

"He is nine years older than you, too!"

"I know! I know! God, I wish it wasn't so. He is so dreamy!"

"Mira, please don't even entertain the thought of being attracted to him."

"Lena, I can't help who I am attracted to or who I fall in love with!"

"In love? You just met him!"

"I know it sounds crazy. I never believed in love at first sight, but oh wow, I do now!"

"Let's go mingle with the other teenagers. You are not in love, you're just awe-struck with your surroundings!"

"No, I am definitely in love with him!"

Mira looked back at Richard and felt that rush of fire burn through her again.

The girls joined some teenage boys and girls that Lena knew from previous years. Lena introduced Mira to them all, although Mira barely paid any attention. All she could focus on was Richard. His tall, lean body with his well-defined muscles. His curly strawberry blonde hair and those icy blue eyes. Was she imagining him glancing back at her? One boy snapped her out of her gaze.

"Do you want to go down to the beach with us?"

"Um, yeah, sure."

They all went down to the beach, and some boys made a fire to sit around. Mira tried to follow the conversations happening around her however, most revolved around the group's memories from previous summers. She heard about the time they took one of the boy's parent's sailboats for a joy ride.

Then one boy lit a joint and started passing it around. Mira, panicking, shot a look at Lena. She wasn't into drugs or drinking. She knew Lena had tried some last summer, and she had promised Mira she wouldn't make her do anything she didn't want to do. Lena took a hit and shrugged her shoulders, passing it to Mira.

Mira felt every eye on her. She didn't want to take a hit off the joint, but she knew if she didn't, it would give these kids reason to question her. She put the joint up to her mouth and drew in a breath. Coughing as she exhaled and passed the joint to the boy sitting beside her. The joint continued being passed around until it was completely gone and they were all stoned. Some boys and girls paired off and went in various directions. Mira's stomach growled and her mouth was dry, so she made her way back to the manor house while Lena went off with some dark-haired boy.

The crowd had dwindled considerably, and there were small groups of guests here and there throughout the house. Mira found the buffet table and filled a plate. Then found some lemonade to quench her thirst. Wandering out into the garden area where there was a gazebo with climbing vines of roses and other flowers, she couldn't identify. She sat down on the floor of the gazebo and ate her plateful of food. She was hoping nobody had noticed she was high as a kite. A man's voice startled her.

"Is this a private party?"

"No, it's the Gardiner's party…"

As she looked up and stared into those icy blue eyes again.

"Why indeed it is my party. May I join you in here, though?"

"Uh, yes, of course."

She stammered. *What is she doing? She shouldn't be alone with this man,* she was telling herself. However, she felt compelled to stay.

"Do I make you nervous, Mira?"

He knows my name! Her heart felt like it was going to beat right out of her chest as he sat down right next to her.

"Yes, I mean no. I mean, you are married."

"You are mesmerizingly beautiful. Did you know that, Mira?"

She couldn't tell whether she was dizzy from being high or dizzy from his flattering words. She couldn't answer him. Her instincts were telling her to run, but the fire in her was spreading like a wild-fire all over her body, making her stay. His scent was intoxicating to her, and she leaned closer to breathe in his heavenly scent. He reached for her face and cupped her chin in his hand, leaned in, and kissed her. Fireworks exploded in her mind and she gave in to the taste of his lips on hers. She knew this was wrong, oh so wrong, but it felt so right. His hands explored every curve of her body as hers explored every muscle of his. He brought emotions to the surface she had never felt before, pure burning desire.

Mira did not know how long she had been with Richard and it startled her when she heard Lena calling for her. Richard was fast at gathering him-self together, and before slinking off so that Lena wouldn't see him, he kissed Mira gently on the forehead and mouthed, "*I love you, Mira. I will see you again.*" She quickly gathered herself and ti-died herself up and met Lena on the garden path.

"Where were you?"

Lena was looking her friend up and down.

"I got hungry and thirsty. I came out to the gazebo to eat and I must have passed out."

Mira lied, hoping her friend would believe her because of her disheveled look.

"Oh, okay, my parents are looking for us. Let me help fix your hair, so they suspect nothing."

"Thanks."

The summer flew by and, as promised, Richard saw Mira again. They snuck around all summer, seeing each other any chance they got. As the end of August drew nearer, Mira knew her time with Richard would be ending. She also knew she didn't have a future with him, although he set up a post office box for her to write to him when she left.

CHAPTER THREE

The assignment

JESSICA AWOKE EARLY SO she could get down to the ferry docks. She preferred to be one of the first ones on the boat so she could be one of the first to disembark. She made sure she had all of her camera equipment and a small overnight bag with a couple of changes of clothes, in case she wound up having to extend her stay a day or two.

One thing she had learned about photographing nature was that to get the right shots, you could not rush the process. She had once camped out in the Amazon rainforest for an entire week just to capture some rare photos of the wildlife. It was worth it to capture the magnificent colors and views. Those photos had earned her some prestigious awards, too.

This assignment sounded pretty tame compared to that one, and she was looking forward to doing a shoot in her backyard, so to speak. She finished packing her car, grabbed her DNA sample to drop off in the post office box, and headed on her way.

The sunrise was bright, so she put her sunglasses on as she pulled out of her driveway. Jessica enjoyed driving, especially when it wasn't in a city. Passing hay fields and cow pastures made her smile. The laid-back atmosphere of the small town in the country that she grew up in and called home always brought her balance. As she drove past Lopresti's farm stand, she noticed their selection of mums and pumpkins and told herself on the way home she would stop to pick some out. She made a quick stop at LuMac's Plaza to drop off her DNA sample into the postal box out front, and as she did, her stomach flipped. There was no turning back now.

By the time she checked in to the ferry and got in line, her nerves had settled a bit. However, she still questioned if she was doing the right thing trying to track down her birth parents. It was more than just wanting to know who she was and where she came from. The knowledge of her being adopted had deterred her from really getting involved in any romantic relationships because she always had this nagging thought in the back of her mind, *what if this guy is your brother?* Not that she didn't have her fair share of dates over the years, but it was hard to settle down in a relationship not knowing her biological family. Also, traveling constantly for work truly hampered any long-term relationships. Her successful career utterly intimidated many men as well. They didn't appreciate a self-sufficient twenty-five-year-old woman. Someday she would find Mr. Right, but right now, that wasn't her priority.

Soon she was driving onto the ferryboat, parking her car, and climbing the stairs to the cabin. She walked up to the snack counter and checked over the menu. A voice interrupted her thoughts.

"What can I get you? Beautiful."

Startled, she looked up and saw a tall, tanned, blonde-headed, green-eyed, smiling young man leaning on the counter waiting for her reply.

"A large hot tea and a blueberry muffin, please."

As she fumbled through her wallet for the money to pay him, she knew she should thank him for the flirtatious compliment. However, she always felt so awkward in these types of situations.

The young man handed her the tea and blueberry muffin.

"Where is a beauty like you going so early in the morning?"

"I am a photographer and I have an assignment out on Gardiners Island."

"Wow, nobody goes out there. It's pretty secluded. You are not only beautiful, but you are lucky also!"

"That's what I hear."

She walked away from the counter and found a window seat with a table.

Jessica loved to watch the shoreline as the ferry left the New London terminal, heading out of the mouth of the Thames river into the Long Island Sound. On the one side was New London, with its mixture of housing and commercial buildings, a once bustling whaling city, now a struggling municipality trying to reinvent itself by attracting tourists. And on the other side was Groton, with houses and businesses, along with historical Fort Griswold, Electric Boat, Pfizer, and Eastern Point Beach. Both towns were much more city than her hometown was and she just couldn't imagine living so close to her neighbors.

As the ferry passed the New London Ledge Light Lighthouse, she recalled hearing the stories of it being haunted. She was more interested in its red and white square architecture and how it was such a picturesque contrast against the blue ocean waves crashing against the rocks at its base with the blue sky that was its backdrop. She took out one of her small cameras that she always carried with her and went outside to take a few pictures.

Seagulls swooped down to the water to get some fish, and Jessica started snapping pictures of their efforts. There were some teenagers out on the deck eating French fries and as Jessica got one seagull in focus, she followed it as it dove down and stole a fry right out of an unsuspecting teenager's hand. She got the shot and then burst into laughter.

The wind was picking up, which gave Jessica a chill, so she went back inside to finish the rest of the journey across the sound. They were passing Plum Island and entering Plum Gut. As the ferry prepared to dock at Orient Point, Jessica got her first glimpse at Gardiners Island in the distance. She had taken trips out this way in the past, but she never really paid attention to the island in the distance. This time, her research piqued her interest even more. While the island had remained in the family for hundreds of years, it seemed to be shrouded in various tragedies, and even one of Lion Gardiner's daughters, who died shortly after giving birth herself had accused one of his trusted employee's wives of being a witch.

Richard Gardiner, who had owned the island with his cousin Alexandria Cromwell, had died at 27 in a sailing accident. It dismayed his wife Mary to find that she had not inherited his portion of the island at the reading of his will and the sole heir had become Richard's cousin Alexandria, who currently owned it. There had been a long drawn out court battle contesting Richard's will, however in the end the will remained in effect. Alexandria had conceded to allow Mary to continue to live in the manor house where she and Richard had lived until she died or remarried. As far as Jessica could tell, she still lived on the island.

Alexandria Cromwell was the last known heir of Gardiners Island. She had married David Cromwell and built a successful real estate company in Manhattan alongside her husband. They had raised three children of their own and her cousin Richard, who became orphaned at a year old when his parents died in a car accident. Alexandria had been twenty-two and her parents were too busy jet-setting around the world to start over raising a one-year-old, so she and David had taken him in. At seventy years old now, Alexandria only had her business and her island now. David and their three children, David Jr. twenty-five, Samuel twenty-one, and Dorothy nineteen, had all perished in the same sailing accident as Richard. She had never remarried.

Thinking about the Gardiner family tragedies reminded her of her losses and the loneliness she felt. She felt a strange comradery with Alexandria even though she had never met the woman. Jessica gathered her belongings and headed down to her car as the ferry docked at Orient Point.

Driving off the boat, she headed toward East Hampton. Along the way, she passed a few antique shops and farm stands. It reminded her of home. She had plenty of time until her meeting at the café, so she took a quick detour to the next antique shop she spotted.

Pulling into the dirt parking lot of an old Victorian-style home. It had an open flag attached to one of its porch pillars and an oak sign with the word Antiques burned into it, hanging above the porch steps. Jessica wondered what treasures she might find inside. She loved antiques and old architecture and this place had both, so she was smiling as she walked up the steps and opened the door. As she stepped inside, she heard a small bell jingle at the top of the doorway, signaling there was a customer entering. A small elderly gentleman with a crooked smile sauntered over to her with his cane. His eyes twinkled.

"What can I do for you, young lady?"

"I am just looking. If I find something, I will let you know."

He nodded and sauntered back to a little counter with an old-fashioned cash register. There was a small stool he sat on and a small old transistor radio playing all the latest hits. The music seemed out of place with its surroundings and Jessica chuckled to herself as she walked into another room. It was filled with antique milk bottles and canning jars. There were various pieces of antique furnishings, a hutch, a dining room table and chairs, an old student desk with an attached chair, and an old-fashioned washbasin.

They filled the next room with books and record albums. She thought to herself, *jackpot*! Her hobbies besides photography were reading and listening to her parent's old record collection. She looked through the titles to see if any caught her eye. Within twenty minutes, she had already found six books and ten albums. She finished perusing the rest of the antiques in all the rooms of the Victorian house and brought her finds up to the counter to pay the elderly gentleman.

"Did you find everything you were looking for?"

The man had lit a pipe that was hanging out the side of his mouth.

"Yes, thank you. I could have stayed in that one room with the books and records all day. You have an extensive selection!"

Smiling, the elderly gentleman nodded.

"That was my wife's favorite room as well."

The man's gaze glazed over as he finished ringing up her order and Jessica could tell that he had become lost in a memory. She understood the feeling well. When she spoke of her parents with her friends, she would catch herself reminiscing about her childhood and then would snap back to reality by one of them shaking her out of the memory.

She left the man in his memory and tiptoed away. As she opened the door and the bell jingled, she looked back and noticed he had snapped out of his daydream. He looked at her and nodded with a smile, and she nodded back as she walked out the door.

East Hampton wasn't far, and she made it there around one o'clock. She decided to just go to the café early and grab a bite to eat. It wasn't hard to find and was a quaint little place with an outdoor dining area with wrought-iron tables and chairs, and an inside dining area with two corner booths and several square tables. As Jessica walked in and sat down at one table, she noticed an older woman, maybe in her mid-fifties, and another woman in her early forties. They seemed to stop talking as she walked in and then leaned in and whispered to each other. Probably sizing up her white t-shirt, blue flannel long sleeve shirt, blue jeans, and work boots compared to their tailored skirts and blouses with high-heeled shoes.

The waitress, a woman about Jessica's age, brought her a menu.

"Can I get you something to drink, for starters?"

"A water and an unsweetened ice tea please."

"Sure thing."

As Jessica waited for her drinks to come, she noticed another sharp-dressed woman walk into the café. The woman took off her sunglasses as she entered, noticed the other two women, and shifted her demeanor from being relaxed to guarded. The older woman at the table spoke first with a wry smile.

"Good afternoon Mary, what brings you to the mainland this afternoon?"

"Not that it's any of your or your daughter's business, Rita, but I have an important meeting later in the afternoon."

The woman curtly turned towards Jessica's table and then halted. After a brief pause, she continued past Jessica.

Wow, whatever relationship these women had, it was definitely not a friendly one. The tension felt in the café was thick enough to be cut with a butter knife. Jessica also felt uneasy as she felt the woman called Mary seemed to be startled by her appearance.

She ordered some clam chowder and a sandwich and continued to people watch as she ate her lunch. Rita and her daughter seemed to enjoy a leisurely afternoon and were engaged in a conversation that only occasionally brought their gaze back to Jessica. Several times she caught Rita's daughter looking at her and shaking her head. Jessica was feeling a little self-conscious. When all the woman's attention, including her own, diverted when a tall man with brown hair neatly combed to one side walked in.

Jessica felt the temperature in the room rise by what seemed like ten degrees as she felt her cheeks flush. She couldn't remember the last time a man instantly attracted her. This guy was definitely in that category. She couldn't tell whether it was his broad shoulders underneath his sports coat, his firm looking buttocks in black jeans, or those emerald green eyes that seemed to shoot right through her when he looked at her. *Wait, why*

36

is he staring at me? Jessica asked herself when she noticed the man staring directly at her.

The man walked right over to her table, which made Jessica feel thankful she was sitting down because she felt very weak.

"Jessica Greenhall?"

Startled that this gorgeous man seemed to know her name, Jessica paused before answering him.

"Yes, that is my name. But, who may I ask are you?"

"Oh, I am sorry. I should have introduced myself first. My name is Timothy Sullivan. I am the journalist writing the National Geographic article you are taking the pictures for."

Timothy seated himself across from Jessica at the table.

"Timothy Sullivan, yes, that sounds familiar. I have never seen a picture of you, but I have read several of your articles. You are very talented."

"Not as talented as you. I have been a big fan ever since the Amazon jungle pictures. That's one reason I specifically requested to work with you on this assignment."

"I am flattered. What are the other reasons?"

"Well, my friend Arthur also requested you. It appears you have more than one fan."

As the waitress came over and took Timothy's order Jessica was reeling with the realization that this gorgeous man who was already making her feel things she hadn't felt in a while was going to be working side by side with her the next couple of days. It was going to be difficult to stay focused on this assignment, with him being a distraction. The two of them had garnered more whispers between Rita and her daughter, making Jessica feel like she was in a fishbowl.

Soon Arthur Brockton joined them, Alexandria Cromwell's lawyer, who would accompany them to the island. Arthur already knew Timothy, so the two men quickly started talking logistics of the assignment while Jessica listened intently. Their conversation abruptly came to a halt when Mary approached their table, sat down, and introduced herself to Timothy and Jessica.

"I am Mary Gardiner, Lady of Gardiners Island and the manor house. Arthur, Alexandria has notified me you and your two guests will stay at the manor house while they do their assignment on the island. I expect my privacy and just know if I had MY way you all would not set foot on the island, but as you know so well, Arthur, I have no say."

The four of them finished up the planning stages of the assignment and then made their way to the private ferry that would take them over to the island. This was turning out to be one of the strangest assignments Jessica had ever accepted. She was going to spend a few days on an island with a gorgeous man, a crazy lady that doesn't want them on the island, and a lawyer in charge of keeping the peace.

CHAPTER FOUR

The secret

MIRA AND LENA RETURNED to school at St. Catherine's, and Mira found it hard to concentrate on her studies. She wrote Richard her first letter.

Dear Richard,

I miss you. All I can think about is our time together, so I can't concentrate on my schoolwork. I know you are married and I know we will never have a future together, but I can't help but love you. When can you sneak away and come visit me?

Love always,

Mira

She mailed her first letter and waited patiently for a reply. It was a week later that Mira received a letter back.

My Dearest Mira,

I miss you too. Even though our love is forbidden. I can not stop thinking of you, either. Next week, I will meet with your father to discuss insurance. I have arranged a tour at St. Catherine's, setting up a scholarship fund. I will drive my Mercedes. On Tuesday at 3:00 pm, I will be there. Can you sneak out of your dorm and sneak into my car? We can go for a drive in the country. I will return you later that evening to your dorm.

Love always,

Richard

Her heart skipped a beat or two. He was coming to see her! He wanted to see her. Their love wasn't her imagination. She sent him a quick note back that she could sneak away with him and she was looking forward to seeing him. She could focus on her schoolwork, knowing she would be in his arms again soon.

Lena had noticed something had distracted her friend and now she had focused again. She figured Mira had just been dealing with leaving her first-ever crush and had finally gotten over him. Even though Mira had a relationship with Richard over the summer, Lena wasn't aware of it. She was only aware Mira had a crush on him. Lena had met a teenage boy named Steven, and they had spent a lot of time together, leaving Mira alone. Lena had apologized profusely to her best friend, but Mira reassured her every time she was okay. Little did she know that when she was off with Steven, Mira had been off with Richard.

Tuesday came, and Mira made sure no one would miss her. She told Lena and other friends she was feeling under the weather and was going to skip dinner and just go to bed. Mira made it look like she was in bed with pillows and blankets, and then she snuck out her dorm window, leaving it open a crack so she could sneak back in. She then made her way to Richard's Mercedes, which she found unlocked and waiting for her.

Richard entered the car and leaned over to kiss Mira. He then started the car and drove them to a secluded dirt road. He parked the car and took a blanket, a picnic basket, and candles, and set them up in the field on the side of the road. Then he went back to the car and opened the car door for Mira, holding out his hand for her to take. They walked hand in hand to the blanket where they spent that early evening together, eating the dinner he had packed and loving each other fully and completely. As they lay on the blanket embraced in each other's arms, Richard stroked Mira's long, curly hair. He whispered as he brushed his lips over her forehead.

"I wish we could be together like this forever."

"I do too. My parents would never approve, and you are married. Mary would never let you or the island go."

Mira looked at Richard longingly.

"When you are eighteen, I will divorce her, and we can get married and be together."

"Oh Richard, she will take you for everything you own."

"It would be worth it all because I would have you."

He passionately kissed her, and all those feelings of the first night together in the Gazebo came flooding back. She would be his forever in two and a half years. They would be together forever. They had a future together. The stars in the sky above them seemed so much brighter, and Mira was content in knowing the man she loved for eternity would reciprocate her love.

It was late in the evening when Mira and Richard gathered their things and went back to the car. Richard drove Mira back to her dorm and helped her sneak back in through the window. Richard made weekly trips to see Mira always using the scholarship fund or talking insurance with Mira's father as an excuse to get away.

Mary never seemed upset at her husband's trips and frequently used those times to go to New York City for the day. She loved shopping on fifth avenue and catching a Broadway show while she was there. Lunch was always at The Tavern on the Square because that was where anyone who was anyone went to eat. She would meet up with friends, both male and female. The tabloids frequently photographed her escapades and plastered the pictures all over their pages with solicitous gossip about her and her absent husband.

Mary loved to be the center of attention, even if it was negative attention. Alexandria warned both Mary and Richard that the negative press was tarnishing the family name and reputation, however, neither heeded her warning. Richard's love for Mira was his focus. He ignored his wife's constant need for attention. Mary, sensing his disconnect, sought connection elsewhere and didn't care about the ramifications.

On one of her trips into the city, Mary met Benjamin Timmons, a wealthy entrepreneur who enjoyed sailing. Their friendship blossomed, and he frequently accompanied her on trips to the city. The tabloids were eating up their friendship and soon rumors were swirling of a romantic affair between the two. This infuriated Alexandria and she set up marriage counseling for Richard and Mary in the name of saving the family name and reputation. Out of respect for the cousin who raised him, Richard agreed to go.

My dearest Mira,

I want you to know I love you deeply and always will. I promise you, when you are eighteen, we will be together. Until then, I need to keep the peace with my cousin and keep up the appearance of a happy marriage with my wife. I am sure you have seen the tabloids and the rumors being spread about Mary and our marriage. While I truly do not care about what she does and who she is with, I care about the family name and reputation. I also care about you, and if the tabloids start following me around, that could be a disaster for both of us.

I love you enough to let you go, for now. We must not see each other for a while.

Love always,

Richard

As she read the letter, Mira's eyes filled with tears. She couldn't breathe. She felt dizzy and nauseous and she ran to the bathroom and vomited. Lena found her resting her head on the toilet bowl and sobbing uncontrollably.

"Mira, are you okay? Do you need me to get the headmistress?"

"NO, no Lena. I will be okay."

"Are you sure? You don't look okay. You look pale, you are shaking, and you are crying."

"I just don't feel well. I will be okay."

"Why are you crying?"

Mira reluctantly handed over the letter and watched Lena's eyes widen with the realization of what she was reading. She then violently vomited again. Lena rubbed her friend's back and sat in stunned silence. Neither girl could talk about what the letter meant. Lena helped soothe Mira and get her cleaned up for dinner that evening at the mess hall. Mira still looked pale when they made it to the table for dinner, but at least she was no longer shaking and you couldn't tell she had been crying for several hours. Mira slowly picked at her dinner of meatloaf and mashed potatoes as her stomach was still feeling queasy. Lena worriedly watched her friend and felt a tad bit guilty for her misery. If she and Steven hadn't left her alone so much this summer, maybe this would never have happened.

That same afternoon, Richard and Mary sat in their marriage counselor's office in New York City. They both played the part of the ignored spouse well and begrudgingly agreed to spend more time together. Mary even suggested they sail together and Richard agreed he would go into the City to see a Broadway play or two with her.

The counselor seemed pleased with the progress they made in their first session. After an evening dinner, they spent the night wrapped up in the sheets together. It had been months since they had been with each other that way and Richard caught himself fantasizing about Mira the whole time and on more than one occasion caught himself almost moaning her name. Mary, who was usually a stickler for Richard using protection, insisted on him not wearing a condom this time, saying she was ready finally to settle down and start a family with him.

Thanksgiving break came and Lena and Mira hugged goodbye as they both went to meet their parents at the pickup area. Lena was worried about her friend. It had been a month since she had received the last letter. Mira had not responded. She didn't know what to say, and she was afraid of the tabloids following Richard and finding out about them. She wasn't eating, though. Lena had noticed her appetite was very poor, and Mira had become very picky about what she ate. She couldn't tolerate pizza. Mira would have one bite and she would go running to the bathroom to vomit. Lena was worried her friend was having an eating disorder. Mira kept assuring her she was fine. She just still had a nervous stomach over the breakup with Richard.

Mary set the table for her and Richard. He would be home soon, and she couldn't wait to share the news with him. She rubbed her belly, smiling. She would always be the Lady of The Manor house on the island now.

Richard sat in his car in the driveway. In the dining room, he could see Mary's shadow. He hadn't heard from Mira since his last letter. It devastated him, thinking he broke her heart or worse, that she hated him now. It had been a month since he sent the letter, 5 weeks since he had held Mira in his arms last. Oh, how he missed running his fingers through her long, curly hair. It was always so silky to touch. Her milky white skin that he loved to taste. And her eyes were a green that reminded him of the ocean. As he thought of her, he became more aroused and he ached to be with her again. He needed to release the sexual tension he was feeling, so he went inside and wrapped his arms around his waiting wife.

Mary felt Richard's arms wrap around her from behind as he nuzzled into her neck and started planting kisses there. She turned in his arms to face him and saw his eyes burning with passion, and she let him take her right there on the dining room table. When he finished, she tidied herself up and then presented him with the pregnancy test with two lines showing.

Richard went numb. How could he divorce Mary in two years and be with Mira when he and Mary had a child together? He had always wanted kids, but Mary hadn't until recently. What about Mira?

His mind was swimming, and he walked out of the room, out the door, and down to the beach where he sat down, put his hands in his head, and mourned the loss of Mira.

Mira walked down to the pharmacy and bought what she had come to get, the cashier eyeing her carefully as she put the item in a paper bag. Thankfully, her father was at work and her mother was at her studio. She could be alone. When she got home, she took the item out of the bag and went into her bathroom. As she waited, she felt a wave of nausea that had become all too familiar the last month. She looked at the item on the counter and saw to her horror the two lines confirmed her suspicions. Turning to the toilet, she vomited, another thing she had become all too familiar with over the last month. *What was she going to do? An unwed teenager, pregnant with a married man's child. There go her dreams of being a lawyer.* What would she tell her parents? She couldn't tell them it was Richard's. This would ruin Richard. She had to tell him, though; he had to know.

51

Dear Richard

I still love you. My period is two months late. I took a test.

I am pregnant.

Love always,

Mira

Richard had limited his trips to the PO Box to weekly the first month after writing his last letter to Mira, although after Mary's pregnancy announcement, he had resigned himself to once a month. When he opened the P.O. Box and saw the letter sitting there, his heart skipped a beat. When he looked at the envelope and realized the postmark was from a month earlier, he tore it open. As he read the words on the page, he couldn't believe what he was reading. Both Mira and Mary were pregnant with his child. What was he going to do?

CHAPTER FIVE

The manor house

JESSICA HAD TO LEAVE her car in East Hampton since the private ferry could only handle one car at a time. Unloading her photography gear into the van that had brought Mary over earlier was a task made easier with the help of Timothy and Arthur. Mary just seemed annoyed at the lot of them. With all their baggage loaded, they all climbed into the van and boarded the small ferry. The crew instructed them to stay in the van while they crossed Gardiners Bay, which made Jessica very uneasy and claustrophobic.

She was never so happy to be docked on land when they pulled off the small, rickety ferry. As they drove the bumpy dirt road that took them up to the manor house, the sight that lay before her took her breath away. She felt transported back in time as the building was a red-bricked Georgian-style plantation home set amongst beautifully landscaped gardens. She could feel the history of the house swirling around her, and she couldn't wait to set foot inside.

"Martin, the butler will show you each to your rooms. He will take your baggage up as well. Stella, the cook, will prepare dinner, which she will serve promptly at 5:30 pm in the dining room. Martin will show you where it is. Betty is the housekeeper and will provide you with towels or any other amenities you might need. Unfortunately for you, we can not provide you with more appropriate attire."

As she finished her speech, she glared at Jessica and looked her up and down.

Martin, a greying gentleman in his sixties, exchanged glances with Stella and Betty as they surveyed their guests and listened to their mistresses' welcome. Stella, a short plump older woman in her fifties, seemed to be intrigued by Jessica and seemed to look her up and down and shook her head as she turned to follow Mary back into the house, shuffling behind. *Probably not impressed with my attire either,* Jessica thought to herself. Betty, a tall, rather gangly woman, turned abruptly and followed Stella. Leaving the three guests with Martin. Timothy leaned toward Jessica and whispered as he nudged her with his elbow.

"I find your attire quite suitable."

Feeling the heat in her cheeks and not knowing what to say back, Jessica grabbed some of her gear at the protests of Martin, smiled at Timothy, and walked into the foyer of the manor house. She could hear the clanking of some pots and pans coming from the back of the house down the hall and assumed that was Stella working in the kitchen. Martin came into the foyer carrying more of her gear and showed the guests up the stairs and to their rooms.

The room Jessica was to stay in had a queen-sized four-poster canopy bed that was covered with a white lacey bedspread and several pale pink throw pillows. There was an oak vanity with an oval mirror on the wall opposite the bed. The door to the left of the bed led to a closet and a door to the right led to a bathroom. The bathroom wasn't fancy, but it had a tub and Jessica could already tell she would soak away the tension tonight.

As she walked back into the bedroom from the bathroom, it startled her to find Betty standing in the doorway to the bedroom.

"Sorry, ma'am, for scarin' you. I was just comin' up to check on if you were needin' anythin'?"

"I am fine, thank you. No worries about startling me, just new surroundings and all."

"How come you not sharin' a room with your handsome fellow you with?"

Betty inquired, raising her eyebrows and wiggling them a bit.

"Oh, Timothy, I just met him today. We are working together, that is all."

Jessica felt her cheeks blush as she thought about Timothy.

Betty turned into the hall smiling as she walked towards Timothy and Arthur's rooms. Jessica didn't like how flustered she got thinking about the gorgeous man staying down the hall. She needed to pull herself together and focus on her assignment. She went for a walk to get a feel for the house and its gardens.

The house was vast, and she found herself a little lost at the end of a hallway. Here on the wall was a painting of a gentleman with icy blue eyes in a tuxedo sitting next to a much younger version of Mary in a blue gown. There was a small engraved plaque attached to the frame that stated Richard & Mary, 1991. Wow, what a handsome man Richard was, Jessica thought to herself. As she looked at the picture, she felt a sense of familiarity, as if she had seen this man before. *Impossible! He died when you were two years old. There's no way you could have ever met him!* She shook her head as she turned around to find her way back to her room.

She found herself face to face with Timothy and bumped into him. Her hands landed briefly on his chest, and she felt a jolt of electricity run through her fingertips. As she looked up at him and tried to stammer an apology, she wound up gazing into his emerald green eyes and noticed the similarity in shape and intensity between his eyes and Richard's eyes. The only difference was the color. That must have been the reason she had the sense of familiarity.

As she pushed herself away from him, she apologized profusely.

"I am so sorry, I got lost and went to head back, I didn't even hear you come up behind me, again I am so sorry."

"I'm not. I was hoping to bump into you before dinner, not literally, but I wanted to discuss some ideas for tomorrow."

Timothy was smiling wryly at her.

"Well then, glad I could oblige you. Let's find a place to discuss those ideas."

Jessica felt more than her cheeks getting warm and she realized his gaze and smile were heating her. They found the staircase leading back downstairs and found a sitting room off to the side.

It had an antique sofa that Jessica automatically recognized as the one Richard and Mary had sat on for the portrait she had seen upstairs. Timothy must have recognized it too and strode over to it and sat down the way Richard had been sitting in the portrait. He reached up and grabbed Jessica's hand as she attempted to walk over to another chair and guided her to sit next to him instead. She laughed as she tried to pose how Mary had sat in the portrait. Sitting this close to Timothy, she felt the heat again. She turned to start the conversation about the next day when he reached over and put his hand against her cheek while he leaned in gently to kiss her lips. The soft tenderness of his lips on hers electrified her.

She felt herself lose control and kissed him back. His arms wrapped around her in an embrace as he pulled her into him. All her senses took over her mind. The feel of his velvety soft lips pressed against hers. His musky cologne heightened her arousal and made her want him in ways she had never been with a man before. The strong, yet gentle feel of his hands caressing her back and slowly moving along her body excited her.

One of his hands moved to the front of her shirt and cupped her breast and she felt a rush of unbridled desire flood through her body as she explored his body with her hands. He maneuvered their bodies onto the sofa and her eyes jolted open and she pushed him away.

"I can't. Not that I don't want to. Believe me, you do not make it easy to say no."

Jessica hastily straightened herself up and fixed her clothes and hair.

"Then don't say no. We can skip dinner and take this upstairs."

Timothy leaned in and brushed her lips with his.

"No, no, no, this can't happen. I am adopted, and I know nothing about my biological parents. I don't know if I have brothers and sisters, especially brothers."

She rapidly explained and trailed off her sentence with pleading eyes, looking right into his.

He didn't seem wounded or dejected like every other man she had told this to. Instead, there was a heavy sigh and a bit of sadness in his eyes, yet she could also see a hint of understanding.

"I understand. All too painfully. You were the first woman I felt I could get through my block with relationships. I too am adopted and know nothing about my biological family or if I have sisters."

Timothy frustratingly ran his fingers through his hair.

"I felt instantly attracted to you though and felt there is no way we could be siblings if I felt such a strong connection to you."

"I am so sorry. I shouldn't have kissed you back, but I felt an instant attraction to you this afternoon also, and I have been fighting the urge to kiss you all day! My DNA kit went in the mail this morning to see if I can find my biological parents or any family connection. Have you thought about sending yours in?"

Timothy laughed.

"Coincidently, I sent mine in yesterday! Maybe in four weeks, when we both have our results, we can resume what we started."

"If we are not siblings, it's a date!"

They discussed their failed attempts at finding their biological parents and found out that the same lawyer's office that had handled Jessica's adoption had handled Timothy's. Similarly, they had lost his file in the fire years ago too. The conversation flowed effortlessly between them, and Jessica felt more relaxed than she had ever been with a man. Discussing the assignment and how they were going to use a hunting blind to get close to the osprey nests so Timothy could observe and write and Jessica could get the best shots. They could agree on rules that she usually had trouble getting writers to agree to. Her top priority was always working in silence. She found it was the best way to get the best shots of wildlife blending in, and he had agreed.

Martin came and found them and showed them to the dining room. The dark wood table and chairs gleamed with the light of the chandelier above. The table had dishes set eloquently, and the food smelled delicious. Timothy pulled out her chair for her and she sat down. He took the seat next to her that was across from Arthur's. Mary was sitting at the head of the table.

"I trust your rooms are to your liking and you have everything you need?"

"Yes, indeed Mary. Thank you. I spoke with Alexandria this afternoon, and she will join us tomorrow evening. She wants to meet both Timothy and Jessica."

"Great! More unwelcomed company."

Mary's response was full of sarcasm as she rolled her eyes.

At the news of Alexandria coming to meet her and Timothy, Jessica grew excited. She had already felt a kindred spirit connection with the old lady just knowing the tragedies she had endured, but also knowing she was a very successful businesswoman, excited her as well. Mary seemed more than annoyed. She seemed angry and scraped her fork against her plate aggressively. Mary made Jessica very uneasy. The woman seemed to glare at her with disgust and disdain. When dinner was over, Jessica went up to her room and took a nice relaxing soak in the tub.

The warmth of the water instantly relaxed her body and drew all the tension from her muscles. She slid down in the tub and tilted her head back while closing her eyes. She heard the bathroom door open and as she opened her eyes; the lights went out. As she struggled to find her towel in the darkness, instead she felt gloved hands on her body, pushing her under the water. Struggling, she tried desperately to release the person's grip. Her lungs were burning, and she started feeling dizzy. She knew in a matter of seconds she would lose consciousness and she would then drown. Someone was calling her name. Someone was knocking on the bathroom door. The person holding her under the water released her and as she came up gasping for air, the bathroom door busted open and Timothy threw on the lights.

"What was going on in here? I heard thrashing. The door wouldn't open, and you weren't answering when I called out to you. Mary will not be happy I broke the door. Are you okay?"

Timothy rambled as he grabbed a towel and helped wrap it around Jessica as she climbed out of the tub, shaking, still gasping for air.

"SOMEONE TRIED TO DROWN ME!"

"Jessica, you are the only one in this bathroom. There is only one way in and one way out, which is through the door that was locked!"

"I am telling you, someone else was in here. They turned out the lights, they locked the door, they pushed me under the water and tried to drown me."

"What's all this racket and why is this door broken?"

Mary angrily came into the room.

"I am sorry, Mary. I broke the door, but it somehow locked without Jessica's knowledge. Jessica wasn't answering when I called her name, and I heard a thrashing coming from inside. I will pay for the door."

"Someone tried to drown me, Mary. I want to talk to your security now!"

Security came and took Jessica and Timothy's statements and said they would give the information to the mainland police in the morning. They reassured Jessica they found no evidence of anyone else being in the bathroom. The chief security guard, Jimmy, convinced Jessica that she had probably fallen asleep, slipped under the water, and had a nightmare that she was drowning because she probably was. The only thing that bothered her was that she knew she wasn't the one that turned off the light or locked the door.

It was late by the time Jessica had settled into bed. Timothy offered to stay in her room with her, and she agreed. He made her feel safe. They talked about hopefully getting the assignment complete tomorrow so they could get off the island. They both fell asleep in the wee hours of the morning.

CHAPTER SIX

The agreement

ALEXANDRIA LISTENED INTENTLY AS Richard held his head in his hands and explained the situation he had gotten himself into. He told her how he loved Mira with his whole heart and truly wished to be with her when she turned eighteen. Alexandria had been calm and understanding. Her demeanor unsettled Richard even more.

"I will take care of everything. I will contact a lawyer friend to put together a closed adoption for the child."

"Will the child be able to track us down when it is of age?"

"We can have that clause put in the adoption paperwork that when the child turns eighteen, the records will be unsealed. If that is what you want."

"Good, I want to know, my child."

Richard helped steer Mira's parents stealthily in Alexandria's lawyer's direction to set up the adoption of Mira's child by introducing them to him at a gallery showing of Kathleen's artwork. The lawyer and the Kennedys quickly became friends. Her parents did not know Richard was the child's father.

Mira hid her pregnancy from those at school by being diagnosed with mono and being homebound tutored. She had told her parents she had gone to a party where a few boys from the St. Joseph's Preparatory school were and had gotten drunk and had sex with one of them.

They pressed her to tell them which boy, however; she lied and said she didn't even remember. This almost blew up on her when her parents wanted to find the boy and charge him with rape. She assured them it was consensual, and she felt the boy was the same age as her, so there was no reason to get the law involved. Her parents agreed to let it go as a teenage mistake when the lawyer found a couple willing to adopt Mira's child. They were also good friends of the lawyer.

Alexandria visited Mary more frequently throughout her pregnancy. The extra attention from her made Mary uneasy. She felt Alexandria scrutinize every detail she told her about her pregnancy, from the morning sickness, to how quickly she showed, and how she seemed to be bigger than her expected due date would actually put her.

One afternoon in late March, Alexandria had stopped by unannounced and surprisingly found Mary's friend Benjamin Timmons paying Mary a visit. As she entered the parlor, she found the two laughing while sitting close together on the sofa.

"Well, what may I ask brings you around here?"

"Mary asked me to come for a visit. She wants me to teach Richard and her how to sail."

Benjamin hastily replied as he got up from the sofa and gestured to Alexandria to take his seat.

"Richard agreed months ago to learn how to sail together. Benjamin is an excellent sailor."

"Did Richard agree to HIM teaching you both?"

"Well, no, but I am sure he will be agreeable to Benjamin teaching us."

"Mary, I don't know what you are up to. However, just know, I am watching carefully and will not let the Gardiner name get tarnished. Take this as a warning."

Alexandria stood up and walked out of the room.

Against Alexandria's advice, Richard and Mary started going sailing with Benjamin every weekend. Richard seemed to really embrace the freedom he felt on the ocean and seeing him happy relaxed Alexandria a bit. As Mary's pregnancy progressed, she stopped going on the sailing trips with Richard and Benjamin. The two men became good friends, which made Mary uneasy.

Mira's pregnancy progressed and Lena came to visit her friend every chance she could get, filling her in on all the gossip at school. Thankfully, none of the gossip revolved around Mira. Lena and Steven had broken up, and Lena was now dating one of the St. Joseph's boys. It did not thrill her parents, as they were worried she would meet the same fate as Mira.

After several meetings with the lawyer, who was setting up the adoption of her child. Mr. Gilman, the lawyer, offered her a file clerk job, knowing Mira wanted to go to law school, eventually. As soon as she recovered from giving birth, she would start working and would work through the summer and during all school breaks. When Richard heard from Mr. Gilman that Mira was going to be working for him, he was happy to know he hadn't ruined her life.

It was an early June morning when Mira awoke with the tightness in her belly. As it eased and subsided, she got up to use the bathroom. As she stood up, she felt the warm gush of fluid soak her legs and feet. Her belly tightened again, and she doubled over with the pain and the realization that her baby was coming three weeks early.

That same morning, in a private birthing center in New York City, Mary checked in, as her contractions were five minutes apart. Richard had gone on a business trip, so he was rushing to find a flight home from San Diego.

Mira's parents brought her to the Day Kimball Hospital, and they admitted her to labor and delivery. Her mother stayed with her and helped coach her daughter through the difficult delivery. She used a wet washcloth and lovingly wiped her daughter's forehead. Part of her felt guilty for making her daughter give up her child for adoption. However, she knew it was the best thing for all involved. The adoption would give the baby a chance at a better start in life. The couple who were adopting had tried to have their own child for years and were unsuccessful. Mira could follow her dreams of becoming a lawyer because of the adoption.

Mary struggled with each contraction. The nurses were wonderful and helpful. They felt for Mary going through the delivery of her child by herself, although Mary assured them her husband was loving and would be there as soon as he could. When it came time to push, Mary bore down and pushed with all her might, however the baby just wouldn't budge and the baby's vitals dropped dangerously low. They rushed her to the closest hospital and into an operating room. They gave her an emergency C section.

Alexandria made it to the hospital well ahead of Richard, as he was stuck in Chicago. He had missed his connecting flight and was trying to get another flight into New York. As she walked into Mary's hospital room, she almost felt sorry for her. Then she remembered how she had deceived Richard and the family for months. It was only a month ago she had found out the truth.

When she had caught Mary and Benjamin in a romantic embrace and had told Mary she would keep her secret from Richard if she would agree to an amniocentesis to determine her baby's paternity. She had agreed, and so did Benjamin. Alexandria was the only one other than Mary and Benjamin that knew the baby was not Richard's. They had made an agreement to never tell Richard the truth. Alexandria slipped paperwork out of her purse, had Mary tearfully sign them, and walked right back out of the hospital without uttering a word.

By 10:00 pm Mira had given birth to a healthy 5-pound 4-ounce baby girl who measured 18 inches long. She held her briefly before the nurses took the baby to the nursery to care for her. It was the first and last time she would see her baby girl. The tears streamed down her face as she grieved the loss of her baby. Her mother held her tight and stroked her daughter's hair.

At sixteen, Mira experienced love and loss that most adults don't even go through. She longed to be in Richard's arms at that moment instead of her mother's, but knew that wouldn't even happen when she turned eighteen. Richard had written to Mira and told her about Mary also being pregnant and that he could not walk away from his child and divorce her. She clutched her mother and sobbed, grieving the loss of both her daughter and her lover.

The next day, Richard walked into Mary's hospital room and gathered her up in his arms. They both sobbed as grief overcome them at the loss of their baby boy. Mary had told Richard the night before when he had called from the Chicago airport that their baby had died during birth. The baby boy had been 7 pounds, 8 ounces and 20 inches long.

They agreed to name him Richard Gardiner, Jr. Mary told Richard she had planned for the baby to be cremated and interned at the family cemetery on the island. He went home that evening and mourned the loss of both of his children. The only consolation was that hopefully when Mira's child was eighteen they would be told the truth about their adoption. With the revealed truth, if they had his name, he prayed the child would seek him out.

Four days later, they laid to rest Richard Jr.'s remains among the family's ancestors. The family, close friends, and, of course, the island servants all gathered around the infant's grave. Mary, dressed all in black in a wide-brimmed hat draped with a black veil, could barely stand without help. Richard sobbed openly. Benjamin, who had befriended Richard through the sailing lessons, embraced his friend and sobbed with him.

Weeks passed and Stella, the cook, asked if it was okay to bring her newly adopted baby to work with her. Mary agreed and swooned over the baby, filling the void in her heart. While Richard begrudgingly agreed, he slowly warmed up to the child.

He took the boy on little walks through the garden, always secretly wishing it was his kid he was walking with. Someday he hoped to walk through the gardens with his child, maybe even walk her down the aisle. He had found out Mira had given birth to a baby girl.

CHAPTER SEVEN

The meeting

THE SUN PEEKED THROUGH the shade of Jessica's window and landed on her eyelids with its warmth. She slowly opened her eyes, blinking the sleep from them. At first she forgot where she was, and then she felt the warmth of the body cradling her protectively. She smiled and wearily let herself enjoy the comfort of Timothy's arms around her. *God, please don't let us be brother and sister!*

She slowly peeled herself out of his arms and quietly snuck into the bathroom to take a shower. She closed the broken door and stared down at it. As she remembered the event of the night before, she shuddered to think of what would have happened if Timothy hadn't broken down the door.

She looked around the room. *How could anyone have gotten in and out without Timothy seeing or bumping into them?* She wondered to herself. There was a window, however, they were on the second story and there was no way someone could get in and out without making a sound. Jessica opened and closed the window, just to be sure. The old window stuck as she pushed it up and struggled to pull it down, confirming there was no way the window could have been an escape. She opened the narrow linen closet. It had shelves with towels, cleaning supplies, and toiletries. There was no way someone could have hidden in there.

Realizing she still had an assignment to fulfill, she took a warm shower, got dressed, and quietly headed down to the kitchen for some breakfast. As she approached the kitchen, she heard voices talking. The female voice spoke first.

"It's eerie the resemblance she has to her."

"Is that why Ms. Mary seems to dislike her?"

She recognized the male voice as Jimmy, the head of the island's security team.

"I suppose, wouldn't you be unsettled if someone who looked like your deceased husband's lover was staying under your roof?"

Wait? Who are they talking about? Who looks like Richard's lover? Richard had a lover? Jessica sat frozen in the hallway, listening and processing what she was hearing. *Are they talking about me? I am the only other female staying under her roof. They must be talking about me.* Jessica felt as if they had transported her to some horror story. She was stuck on an island with a crazy lady who was associating her with her dead husband's lover. *What have I gotten myself into?*

Jessica took a deep breath, controlled her shock at what she just heard, and entered the kitchen. As she set foot in the room, Stella and Jimmy both looked startled to see her. Stella rubbed her hands on her apron and started busying herself with preparing breakfast for the house guests. Jimmy brought his coffee cup up to his lips and took a sip, swallowed, then cleared his throat.

"Ms. Greenhall, how did you sleep?"

"After almost being drowned? Just ducky. No pun intended."

"Now, Ms. Greenhall, we discussed this last night. You most likely fell asleep and were dreaming you were being drowned because you were drowning."

Jimmy tried to be reassuring.

"We went over the bathroom with a fine-tooth comb. There was no evidence of another person besides your companion, Timothy, anywhere near the bathroom. By the way, how well do you know him?"

"Timothy? I just met him yesterday. We are working together on an assignment. He is a writer for National Geographic and I am a freelance photographer."

Is he insinuating Timothy was the one that tried to drown me? Jessica thought to herself.

"Do you usually sleep with strange men the first time you meet them?"

Jimmy was peering over his coffee cup at Jessica.

Jessica was getting furious at his line of questioning. She needed a cup of tea and some food.

"Not that my personal life is any of your business, but no, I normally do not sleep with strange men the first time I meet them. After he saved me from a near death experience though, I felt safer with him near me while I slept."

Briskly answering the question, then she turned to Stella.

"Could I please have a cup of tea and may I ask when breakfast will be served?"

"Why, of course dear, I will pour you a cup of tea, and I will serve breakfast in about 20 minutes. My Jimmy doesn't mean you any harm or to upset you. He is just asking you questions and looking at all angles like a good detective would."

Jimmy finished his coffee, put his cup in the sink, kissed Stella on top of the head, and walked out of the kitchen.

"Your Jimmy?"

"Yes, my husband and I adopted him twenty-five years ago. He is such a good boy. He grew up on this island and now he protects it and everyone who lives here."

Stella handed Jessica her tea and brought her sugar and creamer to put in it. Jessica thanked her and took her tea with her while she went outside to walk in the gardens. She couldn't help feeling unsettled after overhearing the conversation between Stella and Jimmy. Jimmy's line of questioning towards her also unnerved her. *How could he even suspect Timothy as the one who tried to hurt her? Timothy saved her, didn't he? Maybe I was sleeping? Maybe I was drowning and dreaming someone else was drowning me? Sounds more plausible than Timothy trying to.* She had so many thoughts running through her head. *At least I know why crazy Mary dislikes me. I remind her of Richard's lover.* Jessica chuckled at that one.

As she strolled through the gardens, she came across a gazebo covered in dying vines. She imagined in spring and summer the vines had flowers that bloomed from them, however the breezes of fall were now rustling the dying leaves. She sat down in the gazebo and sipped her tea in the peacefulness.

"There you are. I have been looking all over for you!"

Timothy came striding over to Jessica in the Gazebo and took a seat next to her.

Her heart skipped a couple of beats, and she felt that warm feeling washing over her again. She took a deep breath and tried to keep her composure around him.

"I am sorry. I got up early and didn't want to disturb you. After you saved me last night, I figured letting you sleep was the least I could do."

"I forgive you."

He leaned over and kissed her forehead.

The warmth of his lips on her forehead brought back the rush of feelings from the previous afternoon in the parlor, and she struggled not to throw her arms around his neck and kiss him on the lips passionately. Instead, she abruptly stood up, spilling the rest of her tea, and explained they needed to get going to set up for the photo shoot and his article.

They both awkwardly sat through breakfast with Mary and Arthur. Arthur said that Alexandria would be there this afternoon to meet with Jessica and Timothy. Mary seemed to seethe with anger towards Alexandria and she seemed to shoot daggers at Jessica every time she looked at her.

After breakfast, Martin brought them out to the barn where there were ATVs that they could use to get around the island. Timothy packed their gear on two of them, and Jessica helped make sure everything was secure. Martin introduced them to a man named Samuel, who was to show them to the osprey nests.

Samuel walked with a limp and had visible burn scars on his hands and face. He also seemed to look at Jessica with disdain. *What is it with everyone on this island? Why do they all seem to dislike me?* She wondered to herself.

They all climbed on their ATVs and headed out to set up their observation camp. They had been on one trail for about five minutes when Jessica's ATV sped up. It only took her seconds to realize the throttle was stuck, as she swerved to avoid hitting Samuel in front of her and tried throwing it in park while turning it off simultaneously. She found herself and the ATV tipping over and rolling down a hill.

As she lay at the bottom of the hill with the ATV next to her and thankfully not on top of her, she took an assessment of herself and if she had any serious injuries.

She looked up the hill and saw both Timothy and Samuel sliding down it to see if she was okay. The look of absolute terror on Timothy's face melted her heart and made her smile.

"I'm okay!"

"Are you sure? Don't move until we can make sure."

Timothy demanded as he reached her.

"Hmf, a woman shouldn't be driving ATVs."

Samuel was mumbling as he stepped over Jessica and went to the ATV to assess the damage.

This infuriated Jessica and even though Timothy was trying to make sure she was okay, she gingerly stood up, walked over to Samuel and the

ATV, and made sure none of her equipment had broken.

"For your information, Samuel, I ride an ATV at home almost daily on my fifty acres of land, where I also hunt and fish. The throttle stuck on this ATV. You could have been on it or Timothy."

Jessica looked Samuel straight in the eyes with an edge of annoyance in her voice.

"Are you sure you are okay?"

Watching her roll the ATV left Timothy visibly shaken.

"I am fine, really, just a little bruised and sore. Let's get my equipment up the hill and on the other ATV. I am going to have to ride with you the rest of the way. Let's get this assignment over with so we can get off this godforsaken island."

"I don't mind sharing my ATV with you. I like your arms around me."

Timothy smiled as he helped her and the equipment up the hill. Jessica laughed as they put her equipment on the other ATV and went on their way. As she wrapped her arms around Timothy and leaned her head against his back, she felt her heart race again and she struggled to keep her composure.

They set up their camp for the day by the osprey nests and worked in silence as they had both agreed upon the day before. They worked well together, respecting each other's craft. Jessica felt she was getting some amazing shots. They ate the lunches Stella had packed them and as the day went on, Jessica felt her muscles ache more and more from the tumble with the ATV.

What is it with this place? Two days in a row, I have had near-death experiences. Jessica was feeling a little paranoid. She wanted to finish the assignment and get off this island tonight. She looked over at Timothy, who was observing the osprey and writing fervently. He was so handsome, and it mesmerized her watching him. As he wrote, she noticed he bit his bottom lip in concentration. She couldn't help but think that just looked so sexy. She sneakily took some photos of him like this as he worked.

It was about 4:00 when they both agreed they had what they needed and they packed up the

ATV and headed back to the manor house. When they got back, Timothy insisted on unpacking the equipment and told Jessica to go rest. As she headed into the house, Jimmy met her.

"Samuel says you had an ATV accident."

"Yeah, the throttle stuck."

"Sure, it was an accident. Samuel says your companion Timothy was over by the ATVs and was the one who packed the gear."

"You are insane. Timothy wouldn't want to hurt me."

"He seems to luck out whenever you have bad luck. I saw how you were holding on to him as you rode in on his ATV, and the grin on his face."

Annoyed with his insinuations again about Timothy, she pushed past him and headed to her room to get cleaned up for dinner. When she got to her room, it startled her to find a dress and matching shoes lying on her bed. There was a note with it.

Dear Jessica,

Please wear these gifts for dinner tonight.

Regards,

Alexandria

Wow, Alexandria is here, and she brought me a dress amazingly in my size, Jessica thought to herself.

Jessica soaked in the tub, with her eyes wide open this time. She couldn't help but feel as though she was being watched. As she got out of the tub and dried off, she tried to shake the unsettled feeling that was creeping back over her. For two days she experienced near-death accidents. *Were they accidents, though? Why is Jimmy trying to implicate Timothy in these accidents? Could Timothy really be trying to hurt me? He was there both times. He knew who I was and what I looked like. Could he be a crazy stalker? Could I have angered him by rejecting his advances?* Her mind swirled with questions, and she wondered if Jimmy was right about Timothy.

Slowly she got into the emerald green cocktail dress that had been on her bed. It fit like a glove. The dress had long sleeves, which she was thankful for because they covered the bruises from her earlier accident. She put on some makeup and pinned up her hair in a messy bun. She pulled a few curls down to frame her face. Jessica couldn't remember the last time she dressed up like this and she felt a little out of place.

There was a knock on her bedroom door, and she went to answer it. As she opened the door, it took her breath from her. Timothy stood before her in a black tuxedo. He stood there looking her up and down and let out a whistle.

"I see Alexandria gave you a gift as well. You look better in yours, though."

"No, Timothy, you look absolutely stunning."

She felt the blush spreading over her cheeks.

He offered her his arm as he escorted her down to dinner. Alexandria made sure Arthur was in a tux as well. While Mary was in a cocktail dress. Timothy pulled the chair out for Jessica and then sat down next to her again. Mary was not sitting at the head of the table tonight. Arthur explained Alexandria would join them momentarily. She was getting a briefing on the incidents that had happened the last two days.

When Alexandria entered the room, she was wearing a silver cocktail dress that matched her silver-grey hair. She looked eloquent and stunning for a woman in her seventies. As she came into the room, she was smiling. She came right over to Jessica and gave her a hug.

"I am so sorry you have had the experiences you have had here on the island. I hope you are okay, and I hope you will not hold it against us."

There was genuine sincerity and compassion in her voice.

"I am sure Jimmy told you they were just accidents. I am fine though, thank you for asking. Also, thank you for the beautiful dress."

"You are welcome, my dear. I am just glad you are okay."

Jessica felt that comradery with Alexandria and as they chatted through dinner, it appeared Alexandria felt connected with Jessica as well. She asked Jessica about her childhood and about her parents and she seemed very interested in her adoption. Mary seethed with anger the more Jessica talked about her life.

Alexandria pulled Timothy into the conversation also, and her interest in him being adopted piqued her curiosity even more. It shocked Jessica, though, when Timothy said his birth date was June 7th, 1992. That was her birth date also! They hadn't discussed that the day before. Alexandria was very interested in the fact they were born on the same day. They were born in different hospitals, though, in different states. She was born in Connecticut and he had been born in New York. This was good news in Jessica's mind. The chances of them being related were very slim.

Mary seemed to come out of her angry mood and slipped into a glazed stare into her plate at the mention of June 7th. Jessica thought she glimpsed a tear in her eye before she abruptly excused herself from the table and said she was going to bed.

After dinner, Jessica realized it was too late to take the small ferry back across to the mainland and she would have to spend another night on the dreadful island. The only consolation was she would spend another night with Timothy. They excused themselves from the table, and Timothy escorted her upstairs to her room.

Timothy closed the door behind them and locked the door. He turned to Jessica, wrapped his arms around her waist, and drew her towards him. She relaxed at his embrace and leaned into him, and kissed his velvety lips. He returned the kiss with passion and fire burning through his veins. He scooped her up in his arms and carried her over to the bed, where he gently placed her down. They embraced each other and explored each other's bodies with their hands while passionately kissing.

As they removed each other's clothes, they heard a scream and a thud. Scrambling to fix their clothing, they got up and ran to where they found Alexandria bleeding from the head at the bottom of the stairs. They immediately called for help and applied direct pressure to the wound. They life-flighted her off the island to the nearest hospital. Jimmy and Arthur left the island to be with Alexandria and to see how bad her injuries were.

It visibly shook both Jessica and Timothy up with all the evening's events. They went back to Jessica's room, got cleaned up, and then just held each other until they fell asleep.

CHAPTER EIGHT

Status quo

RICHARD AND MARY STOPPED going to marriage counseling. Mary slipped into a deep depression after losing their child. The only time she seemed to come back from her depths of despair was when Stella brought her baby around. The little baby boy would snuggle into her arms as she rocked him to sleep and she would hold him for however long he napped. Stella didn't seem to mind the amount of attention Mary gave the little one. When the baby wasn't around, Mary was miserable with everyone, including Stella.

Benjamin resumed the sailing lessons with Richard. Richard tried to be there for Mary and tried to be a loving husband. He begged her to come sailing with him and Benjamin to get her out of the house and back into living life. She finally agreed and the more and more she went, the happier she seemed to be.

After a few weeks, Mary seemed to come out of her depression. Richard tried rekindling the romance in their relationship. He brought her flowers, took her into the city for a Broadway play, and took her out to dinner at her favorite restaurant. When they got home, he led her up the staircase to their bedroom and gently kissed her. She pulled away, went into the bathroom, and got ready for bed. This frustrated Richard. It had been months since he had made love to his wife and even longer since he had been with Mira.

The thought of Mira made him hunger for her touch. He went for a walk down by the beach. Sitting there in the darkness listening to the waves crash upon the shore, he decided he would send a letter to Mira. He was sure she wouldn't respond. *Why would she? I ruined her life before it even really began. I broke her heart.* He missed her, loved her, and wanted to be with her. He had to tell her exactly how he felt and let the chips fall where they may.

Mira had recovered from giving birth and was working at the law office as a file clerk. She was a quick learner and soon was also covering for the receptionist and helping some secretaries with letters that needed to be typed. Downstairs in the file cabinet room, as she filed away files, she came across a file with her name on it.

She knew she shouldn't open it, however, curiosity got the best of her. It was the file regarding her daughter's adoption. It had all the information in it, who adopted her, and where they lived. Her heart ached thinking about her daughter, and a tear rolled down her cheek. Mira wiped it away and made copies of everything in the file. She didn't know what she was going to do with the information. Mira wanted the information to keep for her own records.

Mira continued with her work filing and came across another familiar name. Mary Gardiner. *It couldn't be. Why would Richard's wife have a file here?* She thought to herself. Mira slowly opened the file and realized it was adoption records, just like hers, except the birth certificate listed the father and it wasn't Richard. When she saw the birth date, her hand went up to her mouth in shock. Her heart broke for her ex-lover. His wife had made him believe their child had died. In reality, she had given the child up for adoption to cover her infidelity. She missed Richard and still loved him. She made copies of Mary's file as well.

When she got home, she hid the copies she had made in a shoebox in her closet. She took a walk that night and tried to figure out what she should do with the information she had. Her mind was swirling even when she got back and went to bed. She needed to talk to Richard.

Mira opened the mailbox a week later and saw the P.O. Box return address. It shocked her. She ran upstairs to her bedroom to read the letter. Tears streamed down her face as she read the letter. He still loved her and she hadn't even told him what she knew about his wife.

Dear Mira,

I know I have no right to contact you because I know I hurt you and our child. I feel like I have lost everything that I ever really cared about or loved. You, our baby, and my son. I still love you and I always will. I would give up everything to be with you again. Mary doesn't love me and I don't love her. I can come to see you anytime.

Love you always,

Richard

She knew she had to tell him. It had to be done in person, though. He needed to see the information she had for himself. She sat down and wrote him a letter in response.

Dear Richard,

I forgive you and I still love you too! I need to see you.

Love you always and forever,

Mira

Richard checked the P.O. Box daily and held his breath each time. A few days went by and he was nervous when he saw Mira had sent him a letter back. As he opened the letter, he took in a big breath and braced himself for her response. When he read the words she wrote, his heart burst with joy. Over the next few weeks, Mira and Richard resumed their love affair. They renewed their commitment to get married. After Mira turned 18, Richard would file for divorce. They were careful not to get caught and in the meantime, Richard never let Mary know he knew the truth about their child.

Mary continued the sailing lessons with Benjamin, even when Richard couldn't join them. Without Richard there, Benjamin and Mary resumed their affair. For appearances, especially around Alexandria, Richard and Mary played the part of a loving married couple. Mary didn't care that Richard was taking more and more business trips out of town, since it gave her the opportunity to spend time with Benjamin.

On one of Richard's business trips, he orchestrated a get together with Glen and Noreen Greenhall. He had set up the meeting under the pretense of buying a piece of their property. The Greenhalls were a delightful couple, and they quickly felt comfortable with Richard. They decided they did not want to subdivide their property of fifty acres. However, they did own another lot down the road that they agreed to sell him.

At the closing, they had to bring their daughter with them because they couldn't find a babysitter. Richard, being compassionate and empathetic, asked his lawyer if it was okay if his file clerk could watch the Greenhall's daughter for them during the closing. He agreed it would be the best for all involved. They introduced the Greenhalls to Mira, and Mira took their daughter into the other conference room.

Mira closed the door to the conference room, and she showered the baby, her baby, with hugs and kisses. The tears rolled down her cheeks. She hadn't seen her daughter since the day she was born. The 9-month-old had little red-haired curls and green eyes, just like she did. The baby laughed and giggled as Mira played with her.

After about an hour, Richard entered the room where Mira and the Greenhall's baby were. He quickly closed the door and scooped the baby up and hugged her. Mira stood up, and Richard pulled her close. The baby squirmed and giggled.

"Someday, I promise we will be a family again."

Richard whispered to them both as he turned and brought the baby back to the Greenhalls.

Summer quickly came, and it was time for Richard and Mary to host their annual start of summer-party at the manor house. An invitation went out to Mira's parents, along with Mira herself. Richard also had befriended the Greenhalls and invited them and their now one-year-old daughter. Mary spent most of her time chasing after James, Stella's one-year-old, and didn't notice the time Richard spent doting on the Greenhall's daughter. She also didn't notice how her husband orchestrated for Mira to babysit the Greenhall's daughter for the day.

Mira held her daughter's hand and walked her through the gardens to the Gazebo covered in flowering vines. Shortly, Mary and James joined them, who were also walking through the gardens.

"What is your daughter's name?"

"She isn't mine. She is the daughter of the Greenhalls. Her name is Jessica."

Her words stung her heart as she spoke them.

"Oh, I just assumed she was yours. She looks just like you."

"It's okay. How old is your son?"

"Oh, he isn't mine. He is our cook's son. He is just a year old, though."

"Wow, they are roughly the same age then."

Mary got bored with talking to Mira and walked James back to the house. This relieved Mira. She didn't enjoy being anywhere near Mary. Richard made his way through the gardens and found Mira and Jessica playing in the gazebo. The memories of the first night he met Mira two years ago and their first encounter in the gazebo came flooding back to him. He sat down with the two loves of his life and put his head on Mira's shoulder. She gave his forehead a quick kiss and then got up to bring Jessica back to the Greenhalls. She knew being seen together would ruin all their plans.

As the months passed by, Richard gathered evidence of Mary's infidelity. He knew he couldn't use the information Mira had found without getting her in trouble. His goal was to file for divorce in April so that when Mira turned 18 in May and graduated in June, they could get married by the end of the summer. He couldn't wait to start their lives together.

CHAPTER NINE

The revelation

JESSICA AWOKE AND REALIZED Timothy had already gotten up. She felt a little dejected that he wasn't lying next to her. As she moved to get up, her whole body reeled from the pain she felt. She quickly remembered the accident she had the day before and cringed as she gingerly got herself out of bed. The shower felt good, and she almost didn't want to get out, except the sooner she got out and got dressed, the sooner she could leave this place.

When she had gotten dressed, she packed up her overnight bag. She put the dress and shoes in the dress bag. As she did so, her thoughts went to Alexandria. She hoped she was okay. The fall that Alexandria had taken the night before still terrified her. Seeing her frail crumpled body at the bottom of the stairs and her head bleeding was a sight she knew would take a while to get out of her mind.

Making her way downstairs for breakfast, it alarmed her to find State Police officers at the bottom of the stairs taking pictures. She stopped midway on the stairs, not knowing if it was okay to come down, and looked over to see Timothy talking to one officer. He caught her gaze, smiled, and gestured for her to come over. The officer looked up also, nodded, and gestured for her to come over. She excused herself past the officers taking pictures and joined Timothy.

"Jessica, this is Officer Stanton. Alexandria is alive. She has several broken bones and a severe concussion. She is claiming someone pushed her down the stairs last night. That is why the police are here investigating. They need a statement from you, and then we are free to leave the island."

"Thank God she is alive! Why would anyone want to hurt her? I will do whatever I can to help with the investigation."

Jessica and Officer Stanton went into the parlor, where he asked her where she was when Alexandria had her accident. If she was with anyone else, and if she had heard or seen anything unusual leading up to Alexandria's accident. She felt her cheeks blush as she recalled what she and Timothy were doing when the accident occurred. She felt bad that she couldn't provide any pertinent information. Officer Stanton also asked her about the two incidents she had while on the island and she gave him all the information about what had occurred. When they finished, Jessica joined Timothy in the dining room for breakfast.

Timothy stood up and pulled out the chair next to him for Jessica to sit in. Arthur was still at the hospital with Alexandria and Mary had not yet come downstairs. Stella served them both breakfast and somberly walked out of the room. Jessica broke the silence.

"I still can't believe someone would try to hurt Alexandria."

"I can't either, or why anyone would want to hurt you."

"Well, I overheard yesterday morning that I look like our ungracious hostess's dead husband's lover. So that's why she seems to hate me. However, I don't think that would make her want to kill me."

"WOAH! Richard Gardiner had a lover? AND she looked like you? YOU'RE adopted, Jessica. You told her that the first night we were here. That gives her a plausible motive. You could be her dead husband's daughter."

Timothy pushed back his chair and ran his fingers through his hair.

Jessica dropped her fork on her plate as Timothy finished his statement. She was shocked. The thought of her being Richard Gardiner's daughter never crossed her mind. It made sense why Mary seemed to hate her. *Would it be enough for her to want to kill her, though?* Her mind was still swirling when Mary entered the dining room, looking quite distressed.

Stella followed her in and helped her get seated at the head of the table. *Could this frail-looking woman actually be a sociopath capable of attempted murder?* Jessica quietly observed Mary. Mary was shaking. She seemed mentally distraught and physically weak. *No, there is no way she could have been the one who attempted to drown me in the tub the first night I was here. Besides, she wouldn't have had time to change clothes before coming into the bathroom. She would have been soaking wet from the struggle I gave. When Timothy and I are alone, I need to remind him of that fact;* she thought to herself. Mary was the one to break the silence after she regained a bit of composure.

"I assume you two will leave promptly after breakfast."

"Absolutely! We want to leave before another tragic accident befalls anyone."

Timothy replied while side glancing at Jessica.

"I may not like having company on my island. However, I assure you, I dislike the fact that there have been three accidents in the two days you have been here. It's very unsettling."

"I know it's been unsettling for me, being involved in two of the accidents. Why is it so unsettling for you? You have made it clear from the start of your disdain for me. It was very clear about your dislike of Alexandria. So why would you care what happens to us?"

"Well, my dear, yes, it's true there is no love lost between Alexandria and me. However, a little known fact is, when she dies, the island will revert ownership over to the town as a nature preserve and I can no longer live here."

"So you don't care about Alexandria, you just care about losing your home?"

They could hear the disgust in Timothy's voice.

"What about me? Why do you hate me so much? I have never met you in my life."

"I don't hate you. You just remind me of the person who stole everything I ever loved and cared about."

Jessica briefly felt sorry for Mary. It must have been devastating to find out her husband had an affair. She couldn't imagine the betrayal she must have felt.

"I am sorry that I remind you of someone that hurt you. Please realize I am not that person."

"I know you are not her. I do not know whether you are her daughter, though. And I do not know if you are my husband's daughter. All I know for sure is my husband filed for divorce a month before his tragic accident. It wasn't until after his death I found out he had changed his will and had taken me out of it. When I went through his things, I found a picture of his mistress. You look so much like her. Remarkably."

"I hate to ask. Do you still have the picture?"

"Actually yes. It's in rough shape. Many times I have attempted to get rid of it. I always change my mind. I don't know why I torture myself."

Getting up from the table, Mary left the room to retrieve the photograph. Jessica looked at Timothy, who seemed astonished at the frank discussion that the two women had just had.

"I don't think she is the one who tried to drown me. They hurt her. However, I don't think she is a psychopath. She has no motive to hurt Alexandria either if what she says about the island being turned over to the town is true. Besides, she wasn't wet the night of my almost drowning."

"She may not have been the one to physically hurt you, but she could have put someone else up to it. She still has a motive for not wanting you alive, right?"

"Does she really have a motive? If I am Richard's daughter, that makes me the one legal heiress to this island. Even if I die, and Alexandria dies, she loses her home. It makes no sense. I understand her anger towards me if I am her husband's daughter. I don't think that would make her want to kill me, though."

"True."

Mary entered the room holding a small photograph that definitely looked beaten up. She handed the photo to Jessica, who covered her mouth as she looked in awe at the woman in the photograph. They could be twins! It was a school photo and on the back, there was cursive writing. It stated:

To my love Richard,

Here is my senior portrait. I can't wait till we can be together forever.

Love always, Mira

(1994)

Jessica noticed the date, two years after she was born. *Could they have carried on an affair behind Mary's back for over two years?* The more she looked at the picture, the more the woman in it seemed oddly familiar. Besides looking like her twin, Jessica felt she had met her before. *There is no way I could have met her before,* she told herself. She realized it was the same familiarity she felt about the portrait of Richard upstairs. *No way, there is no way I could have known these two people,* she thought as she shook her head.

"Penny for your thoughts?"

Timothy could see the pensive look in Jessica's eyes.

"This picture is from two years after I was born. I can understand why Mary thinks I look like her. We are almost twins. And oddly, the woman seems familiar to me, just like the picture of Richard upstairs gave me the same feeling. My adoption was closed. They adopted me a day after I was born. There is no way I could have met either of them."

Jessica continued to stare at the photograph, feeling baffled.

This time it was Mary's turn to be astonished as she sat down and covered her mouth with her hand herself.

"Does this manor house or the gardens give you the same sense of familiarity?"

"Actually, now that you mention it, the gardens and around the gazebo seem very familiar too."

Abruptly, Mary got up and left the room, mumbling something like I will be right back. Leaving Timothy and Jessica looking at each other, puzzlingly. When she came back, she had a photo album labeled Summer of 1993 Party. She frantically flipped through the pages to find the photograph she was looking for. She always had pictures taken at their parties, usually of the different families. Finally, she found the picture she was looking for and placed the album in front of Jessica. Mary sat down and sobbed uncontrollably.

When Jessica looked at the page, two pictures jumped out at her. One labeled the Greenhalls, which had a picture of her and her adopted parents, and the other labeled the Kennedys, which had the young woman named Mira in it. *I have been to this island before AND I have seen Mira and Richard before;* she told herself.

"Mary, are you okay?"

Mary shook her head no and tried to compose herself. When she finally did, she explained how, after Jessica said that she felt the familiarity of the gazebo and of Mira and Richard, it jogged her memory. She recalled how she had been walking with Stella's son, Jimmy, and had encountered Mira with Jessica. She had forgotten all about the encounter until this morning.

"I am so sorry that I have brought up more terrible memories. Can I keep these pictures please? It may help me answer some questions about who my biological parents are. "

"Sure."

Mary handed Jessica the pictures. She closed the album and walked to the doorway of the room. She turned and looked at Jessica and Timothy.

"I hope you find closure. Please let me know what you find out."

Mary walked out of the room, leaving Jessica and Timothy in awkward silence.

Chapter Ten

The fire

THERE WAS A KNOCK at the manor house door, and Martin answered it for Mrs. Gardiner. It perplexed him it was a sheriff.

"May I speak to Mary Gardiner?"

Martin summoned the sheriff into the foyer and went to get the lady of the house. Mary walked into the foyer.

"Are you Mary Gardiner?"

"Yes, I am."

"You have been served."

The sheriff handed her a big manila envelope. He turned and let himself out of the manor house.

Mary stood holding the envelope in absolute shock. She went into the parlor and sat down as she opened up the envelope. Inside were divorce papers. Richard was filing for divorce? As she read the paperwork, it enraged her! He was filing based on infidelity, which nullified her getting anything from him according to their prenuptial agreement. She was seeing red; she was so angry! There was no way she was going to lose her island, her manor house, or her status in the Hamptons.

Richard felt free already. Knowing Mary was being served with the divorce papers made him feel like a new man. He couldn't wait to start his new life with Mira. He knew the divorce would be messy. Alexandria was already furious with him because of the ramifications to the family name this would cause. He had already discussed with her, giving up his portion of ownership of the island, although no specifics were discussed yet.

Mira had gotten accepted into Harvard and she would start in the fall. They were going to move to Boston as soon as they got married. She knew he had filed for divorce and Mary was getting served. She couldn't wait to start her life with Richard.

Mary had calmed down and thought more rationally. She made a phone call and poured herself a glass of wine. After the phone call, she was feeling much better, and she knew everything would be okay. She would not be losing her island, her manor house, or her status among the elites in the Hamptons. They set the plans to ensure her name stayed untarnished in motion.

Richard was thankful he had business trips planned that would keep him away from Mary for a few weeks. He knew her temper, and he knew the divorce papers would set her off. The only thing that disappointed him was he wouldn't be able to see Mira during that time. He missed her when he was away, so he called up Mr. Gilman and made an appointment that afternoon to discuss some legal issues so he could get a quick visit in with Mira while he was there.

At Mr. Gilman's office, he was busy with another client when Richard got there. As he sat in the waiting room, he heard heated voices coming from behind the conference room door. Richard recognized both men's voices. One was Benjamin's, and the other was Mr. Gilman's. What- ever they were discussing, Benjamin was furious. As he slammed the door open and stormed out of the office, he didn't even realize Richard was sitting there.

"Hey Richard, sorry you had to witness that. You can't please them all."

Mr. Gilman walked out to shake Richard's hand.

"Wow, I have never seen that side of Benjamin! I don't think he even noticed me sitting here."

"You are lucky he didn't recognize you. Your soon to be ex-wife sent him to intimidate me into giving him information about who you are claim- ing she is having an affair with. Don't worry, I didn't break and give him any information."

Mr. Gilman explained as they walked to his office and sat down.

The two men sat for an hour discussing the di- vorce proceedings, updating Richard's will, and discussing the possibility of Richard giving up his share of the island to Alexandria.

When they were done, Richard sat across the street in his car until he saw Mira leave the building to go to her car. When Mira saw Richard parked next to her, she smiled and quickly jumped into the passenger seat. They went for a drive to a secluded spot where they could be all alone.

As they passionately embraced, they heard sirens howling in the distance. They looked out the windshield and could see a glow in the sky. Something was burning. Curiosity got the best of them both and they drove towards the glow. Horror struck them as they realized it was Mr. Gilman's office. Flames fully engulfed the building.

Richard pulled up near Mira's car so she could get home before her parents heard about the fire and worried. As he pulled out of the parking lot, he saw a man standing on the corner facing the fire with a smirk on his face and his hands in his pockets. It was Benjamin!

It was then that Richard realized Mary was playing for keeps and would stop at nothing to get what she wanted. He also realized he needed to make sure Benjamin felt safe and make him think he didn't suspect him as Mary's lover.

Four hours later, when he got to his hotel room. He made a phone call to his friend Benjamin. After a few rings, the phone picked up.

"Hello."

"Hey Ben, it's Richard. A friend would be great to talk to. Mary has been having an affair with someone else. I don't know with who. She received divorce papers today. I won't be home for a few weeks. I have business to attend to out of town, but when I get back, maybe we can go on a sailing trip."

Richard smooth talked Benjamin, hoping it would lull him into a false sense of security.

"Oh, hey Richard, I am so sorry to hear that, pal. Definitely, when you get back, we will set up a trip."

Benjamin smiled wryly on the other end of the phone.

"Sounds like a plan. I will call you when I get back to town."

"Sure does."

Benjamin hung up the phone. As he did, he breathed a sigh of relief. Everything was falling into place.

Benjamin made another phone call before he went to bed. He knew he would have sweet dreams of a future with the love of his life, Mary. They would own Gardiners Island together in the end. It was only a matter of time.

Mary went to bed in a much better mood than she had been earlier in the day. She was feeling hopeful about her future with Benjamin. She would have everything she ever wanted or cared about. Her island, her manor house, and her reputation with the Hampton elite would still be intact.

It shook Mira up about her boss's business burning to the ground. Her parents were thankful she wasn't in the building. It was fortunate that nobody was. When she was sure her parents were in bed. She closed her bedroom door and took the shoebox out of her closet. She was thankful she had made copies of the two adoption files when she first found them. Somehow, someday, she hoped her daughter would search for her and she would have all the documentation and proof to prove who she was. As for the other file, it may serve a purpose someday. However, she didn't know how or when.

Richard went to bed feeling free and knowing Mira would be his wife as soon as his divorce from Mary was final.

Chapter Eleven

The visit

As Timothy and Jessica loaded the van with their things. Timothy's cell phone rang. He recognized the caller's number. It was Arthur, and he answered it immediately.

"Hey Arthur, How is Alexandria doing?"

Jessica couldn't hear the response from Arthur, however, she saw the concern on Timothy's face.

"Sure, I can. I can't answer for Jessica though. I will ask her."

Timothy turned to Jessica.

"Hey, Arthur is saying Alexandria is stable right now and is asking specifically to see us. Are you up to traveling to the hospital to visit her?"

"Absolutely!"

"Okay, Arthur, she is up for the visit. Send me the directions to the hospital via text and we will be on our way."

The two of them finished loading the van and then climbed inside. The driver took them to the rickety ferry and across to the mainland, where they left their cars parked. After transferring their things to their respective cars, they took Timothy's car to the hospital to visit Alexandria.

It was going to be an hour and a half drive to Nassau University Medical Center, where Alexandria was being treated for her injuries. That was with no traffic, which would take a miracle out on Long Island. Jessica and Timothy discussed the revelations that Mary had told them this morning. Neither of them could believe that Jessica had been on the island before as a child and that she might have actually met her biological parents.

They both figured that it made sense if Mira was underage that they kept the pregnancy a secret and put the baby up for adoption. What made little sense, though, was the fact the adoption was closed. *How did her adoptive parents end up taking her to the island that summer? They swore they didn't know who her biological parents were. They wouldn't have lied to her, would they?* Jessica's mind filled with so many questions.

She felt so many emotions all at once. Part of her was excited that she might finally have a lead who her biological parents were and part of her was feeling a bit betrayed that her adoptive parents might have known all along. In what seemed like no time at all, they were pulling into the hospital parking lot.

Timothy opened Jessica's car door and helped her out. He could tell she was still sore from her ATV accident. He could also tell the information Mary had given them earlier was weighing heavily on her mind.

"Hey since you are here, maybe you should get yourself checked out with all those bumps and bruises."

"I am fine, just sore. I want to visit Alexandria."

As they walked into the lobby of the hospital, Arthur and Jimmy met them. They both looked equally worried, which made Jessica and Timothy both uneasy.

"Is everything okay with Alexandria?"

"She is still stable."

"Then why the concerned looks on your faces?"

"Well, it looks like I owe you an apology. After your statements to the state police, they went over the room you were staying in. Especially the bathroom. They found a secret door in the linen closet. It led to a ladder that led to the attic. There is a back staircase that leads to the kitchen by the back door that also leads to the attic. Anyone could have snuck into the bathroom, locked the door, and try to drown you if they knew about that passageway. Even after living on the island my entire life, I never knew about it! I failed my job. I am sorry."

Jimmy stammered out his words.

Jessica felt dizzy and reached for a chair to sit in. *So someone was trying to drown her! Who would want her dead?*

"Who would want to kill me?"

"I don't know, but I am determined to find out."

Jimmy looked Timothy in the eyes.

"Also, I owe you an apology. I am sorry. I thought it was you trying to scare her so she would look at you as her hero."

"No problem, man, you were just doing your job."

"Let's go visit Alexandria and we will worry about all this later."

Interjected Arthur, who was anxiously awaiting visiting with Alexandria, knowing she really wanted to see Jessica and Timothy.

The four of them got visitor passes and got in the elevator. Jessica disliked elevators, however, she hated looking like she was weak more, so she quietly kept her anxiety at bay for the ride up to Alexandria's floor. When they got to the room Alexandria was in, it shocked Jessica to see a State Trooper standing outside it. Arthur simply said they were all with him and they could enter.

Alexandria smiled when they walked in.

"There you all are! I have been waiting to see you!"

"Oh, I am so glad you are okay! I was terrified seeing you at the bottom of those stairs last night."

Jessica leaned in and gently hugged her.

"Doctors said if it wasn't for your quick thinking and first aid skills, I might not have made it. I am not out of the woods yet. I have some bleeding on the brain they are watching. That's why I need to talk to all of you. I need to get some things off my chest. There are some heavy family secrets that I carry. I lived my life worrying about my reputation and my family name and now, at the end of my life. I have no family that knows me, and all I have is my reputation. It's a lonely place to be."

"You are going to be fine. You are a strong woman. And just because we aren't blood doesn't mean we can't be family."

Jessica squeezed her hand and tried to hold back the tears forming in her eyes.

"That's just it child, two of you in this room very well might be family by blood. My pride in my reputation and worrying about the family name made me make some choices I regret. After losing my entire family, I have tried for years to find the two children I orchestrated the adoptions for all in the name of saving the family name. What is a family name without a family? I pray I have found you. I fear I am running out of time. If I am right, Jessica, you are the daughter of my cousin Richard Gardiner and his mistress Mira Kennedy. As for you, Timothy and Jimmy, I don't know which one of you might be the son of Mary Gardiner and her lover Benjamin Timmons. Benjamin Timmons was also Richard's half-brother. When I forced Mary to have an amniocentesis, I found out. I had Benjamin provide DNA to prove he was Mary's baby's father. I had Richard provide a DNA sample to prove the paternity of Mira's baby before adoption and to rule him out as Mary's baby's father. That's how I found out they were half-brothers. Richard never knew that Mary's baby was not his. He also never knew that the baby was born alive and given up for adoption. I am the only one who knew Richard and Benjamin were brothers. I know this is a lot to ask.

Can you all provide a DNA sample? I have a lab that will give us the results in two hours."

As Alexandria rambled, Jessica, Timothy, and Jimmy stood there in stunned silence.

Jimmy broke the silence first.

"Woah, that's a lot to process, Ms. Alexandria. I have lived on Gardiners Island my entire life and now you are telling me I might actually be a Gardiner?"

Timothy chimed in next.

"Let's do this. I am hoping I am not a Gardiner. No offense, because if Jessica is a Gardiner and I am too, that means I have no chance of a relationship with her!"

"Well, after the information I got from Mary this morning and hearing this. I want to know, so sign me up."

"What information did Mary give you?"

Jessica and Timothy filled in the others on the information Mary had given them. Jessica pulled out the pictures to show. After seeing the pictures, they all agreed that Jessica was probably Mira and Richard's daughter.

Arthur made a call and soon a lab tech came in to take DNA samples to run. Arthur pulled out copies of Richard's DNA and Benjamin's DNA reports from his briefcase for the lab tech to compare the samples to. Now it was just a waiting game. Arthur, Jimmy, Jessica, and Timothy let Alexandria get some sleep and they went to have dinner.

They ate in awkward silence. Jessica pushed her food around on her plate and barely ate anything. Her stomach was in nervous knots. She was possibly on the verge of knowing who her biological parents were. The sad part was if Richard was her father, he was dead, and no one knew where Mira Kennedy had ended up. At least she potentially had names.

Jimmy tried to eat his burger and fries. He was having a hard time wrapping his head around the fact he might be Mary Gardiner's son. He had known the woman his entire life. *Did she know? Did his adoptive parents know?*

Timothy had his own thoughts running through his brain. He kept thinking there was no way Jessica was his cousin. He couldn't have an attraction to a relative. Then the horrific thought crossed his mind: *what if they were cousins? Did that make him sick because he might have a crush on his potential cousin?* It turned his stomach so much that he couldn't finish eating.

They all got hotel rooms for the night because, by the time they received the results, it would be too late to drive back to the Hamptons and Gardiners Island. While at the hotel, Arthur received a phone call from the lab.

When they got back to the hospital and up to Alexandria's room, the lab tech was already in there, going over the results with her. She had tears streaming down her face. She quickly wiped them away as they walked in.

"Arthur, we must draw up a new will immediately. I am leaving my entire estate, including Gardiners Island to my two sole heirs, Jessica Greenhall, the daughter of the late Richard Gardiner, and James 'Jimmy' Driscoll, the son of the late Benjamin Timmons (Gardiner)."

Jessica went numb. This was the moment she had been waiting for the last six years. She had family. Two members that were in the same room as her currently. What she never expected was to become an heiress to a million-dollar fortune and a private island. She finally knew who her biological parents were!

Jimmy seemed stunned. He knew about his adoption. He never questioned who his biological parents had been. Having the information now seemed a betrayal to his adoptive parents. He couldn't believe he was an heir to a fortune and the island he grew up on, too.

The news elated Timothy! He now knew 100% without a doubt there was no relation to Jessica, which meant he was free to pursue his romantic feelings toward her. He walked up to her and wrapped his arms around her. Taking his cue, she wrapped her arms around his neck and planted a kiss right on his lips. She pulled away.

"We will continue this later in private. Right now, I have a family to get acquainted with."

CHAPTER TWELVE

Charades

RICHARD RETURNED TO THE manor house after a few weeks of business trips to find Mary had all of his things moved to another bedroom furthest from hers. He honestly didn't mind, as he was planning on doing just that when he got home, anyway. All pretenses about a blissful marriage were gone now as well.

Alexandria was furious with Richard for filing for divorce and he knew he was going to have to work really hard at smoothing things over with her. He would talk to Benjamin about that sailing trip and see if Alexandria and her family could join them. Some quality family time might just do the trick.

He called up Benjamin and asked to meet him at one of the local bars to talk. Benjamin agreed and that afternoon they sat there laughing and having a good ole time drinking some beers. Casual observers would have thought they were best friends. They were both good at putting up the false façade.

When they left the bar, they shook hands and patted each other on the shoulder, as good friends would. As each of them returned to their prospective cars, though, they each had a wry smile on their face thinking they had just pulled a fast one over the other.

Benjamin got back to his house and quickly made a phone call. The conversation with the other person was short and to the point.

"We need to meet tomorrow. Usual spot. Usual time."

After, he went down to his dock and boarded his sailboat.

He loved his boat; it was his pride and joy. The twinge of sadness he felt when he thought about not owning it soon crept over him. Telling himself it would be all worth it in the end. He would have something so much better, his Mary.

Back at the manor house, Richard was walking in the door as Mary was heading up the stairs to go to her room. Part of him felt guilty. He knew he hadn't been faithful in their marriage, either. Then he remembered the ultimate betrayal Mary had pulled, making him believe she was pregnant with his child and that their child had died. That was unforgivable.

Mary didn't even look back down the stairs when she heard the door open. She knew it would be Richard. She wondered what had happened to them both. They had been so in love when they first married. They were the talk of the Hamptons and everyone aspired to be like them. Now, they would be the laughingstock, thanks to him and his blasted divorce. Not if she could help it, though. She was still hoping to get out of this mess without a tarnished reputation and hold on to the manor house and the island.

In Connecticut, Mira was helping her boss, Mr. Gilman, set up his new office. It had taken a couple of weeks to find a suitable place, however, he finally found the perfect setup. Mira was just happy to be back working and doing what she loved, learning about the law. They had ruled the fire arson. However, there were no leads. Richard gave an anonymous tip to the police about Benjamin Timmons, yet they had no evidence linking him to the actual fire.

When they questioned Benjamin about the fire, he was very cooperative. He had admitted to having a heated argument with Mr. Gilman earlier in the day. He had also admitted that he had gone back to apologize when he came upon the fire scene. After the police had left him, Benjamin was fuming.

The thought that someone that knew who he was seeing him at the fire bothered him. He had noticed no one who was familiar. He tried to remember back to that day and he tried to remember if there was anyone else in the waiting room when he left. All he could remember was his anger and storming out.

He didn't trust Mr. Gilman, the slimy sleaze ball of a lawyer that Alexandria had forced Mary to work with for the adoption of their son. A son he never got the chance to meet or hold. He had no say in the entire process.

Alexandria had all the proof she needed to take them both down and ruin their lives, yet she hurt them in the worst way possible to save her precious family name. Oh, how he hated her for the hurt she caused Mary. Soon, he hoped he could repay the favor.

On May 2, 1994, Richard made a trip to Connecticut to see Mira. It was a special day as Mira turned 18. Mira had told her parents she was taking the day off and going to the beach as a cover for meeting up with Richard and spending the day with him. They took a small road trip to Newport, Rhode Island, where they figured it would be safe for them to have an actual date finally.

They enjoyed the day as any normal couple would. Holding hands and stopping for a kiss or two as they walked together and did some sightseeing. They toured some mansions and in one garden of Hammersmith Farm, Richard knelt down on one knee and proposed to Mira.

Of course, she said yes. They were so happy together and they both noted the irony of getting engaged at a former Kennedy estate and her having the last name of a Kennedy.

The proposal overjoyed Mira. The gorgeous ring Richard had picked out overwhelmed her. She knew she was going to have to be very careful not to wear it in public just yet. For today, though, she was enjoying being the future Mrs. Richard Gardiner.

On the way back to Connecticut, Richard stopped at a quaint roadside motel and rented a room. They had never shared a bed. It had always been too risky for him to be seen with an underage girl. Now that Mira was eighteen, they were safe.

Before Mira entered the room, Richard set it up with candles, roses, and even a bottle of champagne. When she entered, the romantic gestures he had made filled her with such joy. As Richard shut the door behind them, he stepped forward and embraced her in a passionate kiss. The fire she had felt the first time they had kissed that night in the gazebo raged fiercely in her veins. They spent the rest of the afternoon and early evening wrapped up in the sheets, making passionate love. When they parted ways later that evening, Mira wanted Richard to know exactly how she felt.

"You have made me the happiest woman in the world. Today was the best day ever! I love you forever, Richard."

"I Love you too, Mira."

By the time Richard got back home to the manor house, it was late evening. Mary was already in her room for the night, although little did he know she was not alone. As he walked down the hallway, he heard a male's voice. At first, it startled him, and then he just smiled, because he realized they were getting bold. He eavesdropped on the conversation and he was very glad he did. After overhearing their plans, he had to figure out what he was going to do next. They were playing for keeps, and he had to as well. A few days later, he visited Mira again and told her of their plans. Their plans horrified her.

"Richard, you can't go on that trip! You can't let Alexandria and her family go either!"

"I can't back out of the trip. They will suspect something is up. I am their primary target. I will do my best to make sure Alexandria and her family don't go, even if it means having her hate me for the rest of our lives. Don't worry, we will use their plans to our advantage. It will all work out."

Richard hugged Mira tight and ran his hands down her hair.

Of course, the trip they were talking about was the sailing trip that Benjamin and Richard had been planning on taking on Mother's day. Since Alexandria had been the only mother Richard had ever known, he thought it would be nice to take her and her family out sailing with Benjamin. Now, he had to get Alexandria so mad at him she would refuse to and refuse to allow her family to go. He had to keep them safe at all costs. The alternative was too awful to even think about.

Richard knew all too well how to rile up Alexandria, so he set himself to call her.

"Hey Alexandria, It's Richard. I hope I am not catching you at a bad time. I need to talk to you about my divorce from Mary and the future of the Island."

"Hello Richard, I am kind of busy with the business. What is it now with the divorce? I hope there are no snags and it is quick and quiet. You know we don't need any bad press. Have you relinquished your half of the island totally to me?"

"Well, not exactly. I want to keep my half of the island and actually, Mira and I want to get married at the manor house gazebo as soon as my divorce is final. Mira deserves a big, beautiful wedding. I want to give that to her."

Richard then held his breath for the fury he knew would come.

"What? Are you crazy?? A big wedding, immediately after they complete your divorce, to an eighteen-year-old!! The press will have a field day!! No way, no how!!! And you want to keep your half of the island! What happened to you wanting to live a life of seclusion after your divorce?"

There it was, the fury, the response he knew he would elicit. After a few more back-and-forth remarks and no compromising. Alexandria told him in no uncertain terms would she or her family be going sailing with him on Mother's Day and that if he went with the big wedding on the island, she would disown him.

Hanging up the phone, it satisfied Richard that his plan had worked and at least his family would be safe from Mary's and Benjamin's wrathful plans. He felt guilty making Alexandria mad, and he made an appointment with Mr. Gilman to discuss drawing up legal documents to give Alexandria his portion of the island. It wasn't much for the pain she would experience soon, but he knew it would console her somewhat.

Mother's Day morning came and Richard headed to the dock where Benjamin kept his sailboat moored at. As he walked towards the vessel, he saw Benjamin, who waved enthusiastically towards him. Stepping onto the boat, he saw his three cousins sitting comfortably, ready to set sail.

"What are you three doing here? I thought your mom said you all weren't coming."

Richard's heart raced with panic. David Jr., Alexandria's oldest son, was quick to explain to his cousin their presence on the boat.

"Mom isn't coming, but the rest of us decided she can stew in her anger. We are not missing out on a fabulous sailing trip. Dad is below deck putting his things in his bunk."

Richard felt sick. *No, this is not how this is supposed to go! Alexandria will never forgive me.* He didn't know what to do. He couldn't call off the trip and couldn't contact Mira. Richard felt helpless to stop what was going to happen.

"What's the matter there, bud? You are looking a little green around the gills? Everything okay."

Benjamin patted Richard on the back.

"I am fine. Must have eaten something that didn't quite agree with me."

"Glad you all could make it. It's a shame Alexandria couldn't come. It will be a pleasant couple of days for sailing."

Benjamin finished his sentence and then started getting ready to set sail. Richard knew there was no turning back. He prayed God would forgive him and that someday Alexandria would, too.

That evening after dinner, Richard went to his bunk early, with the pretense of feeling under the weather. The others stayed up later, drinking and playing cards. He couldn't sleep. He prayed the others could.

In the morning, news spread fast about the tragic explosion that engulfed the sailboat, killing all souls on board. It devastated Alexandria, her entire family gone in one fell swoop. Mary was told of the death of her husband and she fainted. Everyone in the Hamptons felt sorry for both Alexandria and Mary. Tragedy always seemed to befall the Gardiners.

CHAPTER THIRTEEN

Family

JESSICA SAT THERE GETTING to know both Alexandria and Jimmy in Alexandria's hospital room until the nurses kicked them out. There were hugs and tears as they said goodbye. There were also promises of staying in touch.

The four visitors went back to their hotel rooms to get a good night's sleep. Jessica couldn't believe the events that had transpired over the course of the last three days. She unlocked her hotel room door and went inside. Shortly after, there was a knock at her door.

It was Timothy. She smiled and opened the door. As she did, he scooped her up, placed her gently on the bed and began making passionate love to her. Jessica lay breathless in his arms. She had never felt so content and happy in her life.

Timothy rolled up on one side and looked down at Jessica.

"Will you marry me, Jessica?"

"What?"

Jessica bolted upright in bed.

"I know it sounds crazy. We only met four days ago, but I know I love you and I want to spend the rest of my life with you."

"Timothy, I love you too. I am just overwhelmed by everything that has occurred over the last few days. Let's take it one day at a time and see how it goes, okay?"

"I will wait till the end of time for you, Jessica."

Timothy sat up, pulled Jessica towards him, and kissed her gently on the lips. Electricity ran through Jessica and she succumbed to round two of passionate lovemaking. They fell asleep in each other's arms.

In the morning, Jessica and Timothy joined Jimmy and Arthur for a farewell breakfast. Jimmy would head back to Gardiners Island to help with investigating the accidents that had occurred. He also had to give the news to his adoptive parents that he knew who his biological parents were. Then there was the matter of confronting his birth mother.

Arthur would stay near Alexandria until her release from the hospital. He would also make sure things at her business ran smoothly while she was away recovering from her injuries.

Timothy and Jessica would head back to East Hampton so Jessica could get her car and head back to Connecticut. Timothy would head back to his place in Riverhead. On the drive back, they would have plenty of time to discuss their blooming relationship and how to make it work long distance. Each of them had very successful careers that could take them anywhere in the world at a moment's notice. It would be challenging, however, they both felt it was worth trying to make it work.

At the manor house, Mary was pacing back and forth in the parlor. The revelations of the day before still reeling in her mind. That Richard was bold enough to bring his mistress to the island infuriated her! Right under her nose, too! She couldn't be mad at Jessica. An innocent victim in all of this. She was also the only potential heir to Gardiners Island if, in fact, she was the child of Richard and his mistress. So Mary needed to stay on her good side if she wanted to remain in the manor house and keep her lifestyle on the island.

Then there was the matter of the phone call from Jimmy about the three accidents over the last few days and the finding of the passageway. He had changed his mind and was leaning more towards the accidents being planned and attempted murder. He would work closely with the State Police. Everyone on the island was being interviewed. She couldn't think of anyone on the island that would want to kill Alexandria. They all knew that if she died, without an heir, they would turn Gardiners Island over to the Town and it would become a nature preserve. It made no sense.

As for someone wanting to hurt Jessica. The only people on the island that knew about her finding the photograph of Richard's mistress were Stella and Betty. They had found her sobbing on the floor the night she found it. They were loyal to her, they always had been, but she didn't think either of them would have hurt Jessica. Did Stella tell Jimmy? Jimmy had been very critical of Jessica and her writer friend, Timothy, the whole time they were here. No, she couldn't see him hurting her, either.

There were other workers on the island and their families. None that she was that close to and would know her business. At least not anymore. She couldn't think of anyone or any reason anyone would want to hurt either Jessica or Alexandria. Just thinking about it all was giving her a headache, and she left the investigation up to Jimmy and the police.

Jimmy walked into the kitchen of the manor house and found his Mom cooking. He sat down at the counter and poured himself a cup of coffee. It was difficult for him to start the conversation about his biological parents. He didn't want to hurt her.

"What's got you stewing, Jimmy?"

She could always tell when something was weighing heavily on her boy's mind.

Jimmy smiled, just like her to always know. She wasn't his biological mom, but she was in tuned to him since day one.

"Well Mom, I don't know how to tell you and I don't want to hurt your feelings. I love you and dad so much. I found out who my biological parents are. It wasn't my idea to find out. There was a reason, though."

Stella dropped the spoon she was holding onto the stove and turned to face her son.

"I knew this day might someday come. I've tried to prepare myself for you to come and ask if it was okay. The expectation was never for you to find out first and then tell us. I am not hurt. You have a right to know where your roots are from. Your father and I know nothing about your birth parents. Ms. Alexandria knew we had been trying for years to have a child of our own and she knew an adoption lawyer, Mr. Gilman. He found us you."

153

"So you do not know who my biological parents are?"

"No, Jimmy. I never really cared much to know. You were ours from day one. The timing was really difficult on Ms. Mary though as she lost her only child the same day you were born. You helped her heal, though. She always loved doting on you."

"Yeah, about that. Mom, I need you to have a seat before I tell you what I found out."

Jimmy pulled out a chair and helped the only mother he had ever known sit down. He then told her everything he had found out. When he told her about Benjamin actually being Richard's half-brother and that he was now one of two heirs to Gardiners Island, Stella gasped.

"Does Ms. Mary know?"

"No, Ms. Alexandria does not want her to know about Benjamin's lineage or that I stand to inherit half of the island. I can tell her I am her biological son, however, until we find out who pushed her down the stairs, who attempted to drown Jessica, and who rigged the ATV throttle to stick, its safer that no one else knows."

"My lips are sealed, Son. I do not want you to be hurt. So Jessica was Richard's daughter? Isn't that something? That's why she looked just like his mistress. It's crazy you were born on the same day, too."

"She is pretty cool, Mom. I guess it's cool to have a cousin my age. Well, I guess I better go track down Ms. Mary and have a talk with her and then get to work."

Jimmy got up, kissed his mom on the forehead, and went to look for Mary within the manor house. He found out from Betty that Mary was up in her bedroom resting, so he checked out the passageway the State Police had found in the linen closet. He couldn't believe he missed it when he did his investigation.

After coming down the back staircase, he headed outside to where they stored the ATVs. The police had taken the one Jessica had crashed on. They wanted to examine it for prints. He found Samuel, the resident island handyman, working on one tractor.

"Hi Samuel, need a hand there?"

"No thanks, kid, I got it."

"How was it around here yesterday while I was gone?"

"Besides the police hounding everyone about those broads' accidents, it's been quiet."

"They weren't accidents Samuel, the police, and now I believe they were intentional."

"That's crazy man. Just clumsy, accident-prone broads, that's all. How is the old bat, anyway?"

"Samuel, I know you don't like Ms. Alexandria. However, calling her an old bat is just plain disrespectful. She is stable. They think she will recover fully, although it will be a long road."

"Good for her. Now, if you don't mind, I work better without distractions."

Jimmy left Samuel working on the tractor and went back to the manor house to see if Mary had come down from her room yet. Martin informed him she had, and she was sitting in the parlor. As he walked into the parlor, he found Mary sitting on the sofa, looking at an old photo album. The album had *The Summer of 1991* written on the spine.

"Good evening, Ms. Mary. May I come in and have a word with you?"

Startled, Mary looked up and smiled at Jimmy. He always brought comfort to her. She closed the album and gestured for him to sit down next to her.

"Of course Jimmy. I always have time for you."

Jimmy took a seat next to her and searched his mind for how to start the conversation with her. Finally, he just figured he would be straightforward.

"Ms. Mary, as you know, my parents adopted me. I just recently found out who my biological parents are."

"Yes, Jimmy, I am aware of your adoption. Your mom and dad have always loved you as their own, though. Why would you want to know who your biological parents are? Aren't you afraid you might hurt your mom and dad with that information?"

"Well, I already told mom. She was surprisingly okay with me knowing. She was just as surprised to know who they are."

"Why are you talking to me about this then, Jimmy? I figured you were coming to me for advice about whether you should tell your mom or dad."

"Ms. Mary, or should I say, Mom, I am coming to you because I am your son. The one that they forced you to give up for adoption because my father was not Richard."

"Oh my. I am so sorry, my Son!"

Mary hugged Jimmy and wept. Jimmy explained how he had found out the night before from Alexandria. She had kept the DNA records from the amniocenteses and the lab could check his DNA against it. He also confirmed her suspicions about Jessica being Richards's daughter. Jimmy kept the part about Benjamin and Richard being half-brothers from her. At this point, he didn't know who to trust. If the island was the motive for the attempted murders, he needed to keep his identity as an heir secret.

CHAPTER FOURTEEN

Memorial service

IT WAS A FEW days after the tragic sailing accident that they held the memorial service for all that lost their lives that fateful day. They held the service at the family cemetery, where they attached an engraved plaque to a lighthouse monument with the names of the dearly departed. There was nothing to be buried since they found no remains.

Mary's attire consisting of black clothes from head to toe, including a hat with a veil covering her face. Alexandria's formal wear was also black from head to toe, minus the hat and veil. Both widows were distraught with grief. Hundreds of mourners attended the service.

Some people who the two women knew well, and others from the community who just came out to support the grieving wives. Many of Richard's friends and business acquaintances attended to pay their respects. Including the Kennedys, the Greenhalls, and Mr. Gilman.

Mira gave her condolences to both women alongside her parents. She also offered to watch little Jessica for the Greenhalls which they were more than grateful for. Seeing her daughter lifted the sadness of the day from Mira's heart. Richard was gone forever.

Lena and her parents were there, too. Lena caught up with Mira and walked with her and Jessica through the Gardens. She felt so sorry for her best friend. She knew with Richard gone, this would most likely be the last time Mira saw her daughter. Mira had told Lena how she had found the adoptive parent's identity and how she and Richard had planned at times to see her under the guise of other things.

As the afternoon turned to evening, the mourners thinned out and Mira's parents were ready to go. She said goodbye to the Greenhalls and Jessica, then got in the car. The long ride home was torturous. As soon as she got into her room and closed her door, she fell on her bed and cried herself to sleep.

Mary, being surrounded by people, was comforting to her all day. She barely could remember all the names and faces. She recognized some. Others, she did not know who they were. Probably business associates of Richards. One such gentleman, she couldn't remember the name he introduced himself as, wore a jet-black suit and sunglasses. He had jet-black hair and his voice cracked as he gave the two women his condolences. He must have been a close associate because he seemed pretty distraught over the loss of Richard.

She tried to seek him out again to make sure he was okay and to find out his name, however; he had vanished among the mourners. Later, she would look at the book that mourners had written in to see if any of the names jumped out at her as his.

Those wishing to comfort her as well surrounded Alexandria. They couldn't believe she lost her entire family in one tragic accident. The more people said it to her, though, the more she had wished she had gone on the trip and perished too. She didn't know how she was going to live without her husband, her three children, and her cousin, who was more like a son.

She, too, couldn't remember the names and faces of all those who came to share in her grief. There was one gentleman that never approached her or Mary. He had stayed in the distance, on the edge of the mourners. Dressed in a black suit, as most of the male mourners had. The only difference was he wore a cowboy hat, sunglasses, a bandana around his neck, and black driving gloves on his hands.

When Alexandria went to look for him to approach him, he had vanished. She would never know who he was or how he knew her family. She was just grateful for the outpouring of support she and Mary were receiving. They were both going to need it to get through their grief. If they ever would.

She had decided it was best for her to stay at the manor house for a few weeks. The thought of going home to an empty penthouse apartment in the city was just too much to bear. Then there was the matter of settling Richard's estate. She knew that would not go over well with Mary. Richard had only made the most recent changes to his will after filing for divorce. She knew Mary would try to contest it.

Mary was exhausted. Mentally, physically, and more so emotionally. She made her way upstairs to her bedroom and soon found herself fast asleep.

Alexandria barely slept and soon the sun came up and it was time to go down for breakfast. She didn't want to get out of bed. Closing her eyes tight, she tried wishing away the nightmare she was living. When she opened them and realized the nightmare was still her reality, she broke down into a sob. She didn't want to live without her beloved husband and children. Why did she let

Richard push her buttons? She should have been on that boat with them all. She should have perished along with them.

Mary awoke feeling a bit refreshed from her sleep. Stella would serve breakfast shortly, so she dragged herself out of bed and got herself showered and dressed. She truly felt sad at the loss of Richard and the others. The only consolation was she could remain here on the island, in her manor house, and keep her reputation intact with the Hampton elites. The divorce never went through. As Richard's spouse, she would inherit his share of the island.

Mira awoke the next morning. She got up, showered, and got dressed. In a few weeks, she would be graduating. Mr. Gilman had helped land her a secretarial job at a law office close to Harvard. On this particular day, her parents were driving up with her to find an off-campus apartment close to both school and work.

She had convinced them she would focus on her schoolwork more if she had an apartment all to herself instead of sharing one or having to live in

the dorm. They were a little leery, especially because of her past. In the end, she used reasoning
to persuade them. She used the fact that for the
rest of her High School years; she didn't have a
boyfriend, she worked, and she received top hon-
ors. It was hard for them to dispute any of it. They
joked she would make an excellent lawyer someday.

When only Mary came down for breakfast, Stella
and Betty went upstairs to check on Alexandria.
They found her sobbing on her bed. They helped
calm her down before they coaxed her to take a
shower and get dressed. When she was done, they
escorted her down for breakfast and doted on her
more than usual. Mary had told Martin she was going for a walk on the beach. They felt sorry for both
women and did what they could to help them in
their time of grief.

Mary came back from her walk and she looked
calmer and less distraught than the day before.
To cheer up Alexandria, she tried to suggest that
she, too, should take a walk down by the beach.
That it might clear her sadness and bring some

peace. However, Alexandria just went upstairs to her room and locked the door.

She didn't want to be bothered and certainly didn't want to walk on the beach and see the water that her loved ones perished in. She didn't want to be coaxed into eating or dressing. Her will to live was gone.

Mira and her parents found the perfect apartment for her. It was within walking distance of the school and her new job. The best feature for her parents was it was a second-floor apartment, which meant less of a chance of anyone breaking in through the windows. They were still nervous about their baby girl living all by herself in a big city. She assured them she was going to be fine. They put a deposit down on the apartment and made plans to move her in two days after graduation.

It took several days before Alexandria came out of her depression. Everyone gave her space to grieve in her own way. Stella had been leaving food trays at her bedroom door at mealtimes. Each day, she noticed that more and more food was being eaten. Alexandria would take a bath daily and when she did, Betty would freshen up her sheets and straighten up the room for her.

It was a Friday morning when Alexandria joined Mary for breakfast. Mary was looking chipper, as if nothing had happened. While Alexandria was still looking like she had gone through hell and back. As Mary finished her breakfast, she left the room and went for her daily walk down to the beach. Alexandria still could not bring herself to go down by the water. She did, though, manage to take a walk through the gardens and to the gazebo.

As she did, she remembered how her children and Richard played in the gardens as kids. They played hide and seek. And of course, their favorite game was to pretend the gazebo was Captain Kidd's pirate ship, and they were pirates. She smiled, remembering how they loved the island and playing amongst the many gardens. It brought her a little peace.

When she went back into the house, she was a bit surprised to see Mr. Gilman with Martin in the foyer. Until she remembered that today was the reading of Richard's will. There was no way to prepare for this. They sat in the parlor and waited for Mary to get back from her walk on the beach. Alexandria knew, no walk on the beach would prepare Mary for what she was about to be told. Part of her felt sorry for her. The other part of her didn't.

Mary came back from her walk, looking even happier than the day before. She sat down in the parlor along with Alexandria and Mr. Gilman and prepared to hear her husband's will read.

"Ladies, I know this has not been a simple time for either of you. As executor of Richard's will, it is my duty to see that I carry his wishes out. This is never a straightforward task. There will always be those who have high expectations that do not materialize."

Alexandria shifted in her seat. She knew he was trying to soften the blow to Mary. Mary seemed to sit on the edge of her seat and was quickly becoming impatient with Mr. Gilman's monologue.

"Can we just get on with it? Just read the will and be done. How difficult of a job can it be?"

"As you wish, Mary."

Mr. Gilman read Richard's will. Mary sat intently listening until he read the Disposition of the property part. *Had she heard that right? She couldn't have?*

"Could you please read that again? I am not sure I heard you correctly."

"You heard it correctly, Mary. Richard bequeathed his share of the island to his cousin, Alexandria. His business and personal assets are to be liquidated and then divided up between you and the St. Catherine's Preparatory Scholarship fund."

"WAIT, I don't get his share of the island? I don't get to live in the manor house? Where will I live? This can't be. We were still married! We did not complete the divorce!"

Mary became irate at the revelation she would lose the island and the manor house along with it. She stormed out of the parlor and out of the house. This was not how it was supposed to be. She wasn't supposed to lose everything.

CHAPTER FIFTEEN

Home

JESSICA PULLED DOWN HER driveway and was so happy to be home. It had been a whirlwind couple of days. On the way back to her car, she had made plans with Timothy for him to come out to her house in a week. They needed to coordinate his article with the pictures she took. The week would give him time to compose the article and her time to develop the pictures.

She smiled to herself, just thinking about Timothy. What a difference it was to feel feelings for someone without the thought of whether there was any relation to you. Finding out who her biological parents were, and Timothy was no relation, was freeing. She thought, *this is what true love must feel like*. Whatever it was, she liked how it felt.

Unpacking her car went quicker than usual, since she had a little more pep in her step just thinking about him. By the time she got every-thing in the house and brought her gear into her photography studio, it was dinnertime. She looked in her freezer and found leftovers she had put in there before she left. While she waited for her meal to heat in the microwave, she put one album on that she picked up at the antique store.

She laughed to herself as the song *You're The One That I Want* sung by Olivia Newton-John and John Travolta from the *Grease* album blared from her record player. She fantasized she was Olivia Newton-John and Timothy was John Travolta as she danced and sang in her kitchen.

Meanwhile, back in Riverhead, Timothy was busy getting to work on his article. The sooner he finished it, the sooner he could see Jessica again. He could not believe how he felt. He had never felt this strongly about any woman before. Then again, he also never was 100% sure he was no relation to any of his past love interests like he was now with Jessica. This was unfamiliar territory, and he loved it. He ordered himself a pizza and once it came; he sat down to get to work.

Jimmy had a pleasant talk with his dad, John Driscoll. He was very understanding and not hurt by the information Jimmy had told him. The man had been the head of security on the island for thirty years. He had just recently retired and was proud that Jimmy had become his replacement.

Arthur sat faithfully by Alexandria's bedside. She seemed to do well, and he was relieved that his friend should be okay. As she was resting, he nodded off, too.

After dinner, Jessica took her film into her darkroom to develop. She still used some old 35mm cameras when she went on assignments along with using the digital counterparts. She found sometimes the older film cameras were better for capturing certain perspectives. This was the most time-consuming process of her job.

She was immersed in her work when the ringing of her cell phone jolted her. Recognizing the name of the caller, she smiled to herself.

"We haven't been apart for more than a day and you are already calling?"

"I needed to hear your voice and also take a writing break. Figuring you might need a pause, too. I know we are both workaholics."

"It is nice to hear your voice, and yes, I probably should take a rest once in a while."

"See, I am already so in tune with your needs."

She chuckled and remembered the night before and said to herself, *Oh; you are definitely in tune with all my needs.*

"Yeah, if you are so tuned into my needs, what do I need right now?"

"Since we are so much alike, I would have to say you are probably needing a repeat of last night."

As Timothy finished his sentence, he realized just how much he really needed a repeat of the night before.

"Ah, you would be correct, Timothy, however we both agreed to get our work done first, then we can meet up."

Jessica paused.

"Ah shit, power just went out."

"Jessica, are you okay?"

"Yes, just a typical Preston power outage. Hang on while I go outside and start my generator."

"Okay, take the phone with you just in case."

"In case of what? I do this all the time."

"Jessica, please."

"Okay, okay. Not sure what the fuss is all about."

Timothy listened intently as Jessica made her way through her back door and outside. As she walked, he could hear her breathing. He could hear her put the phone down. He heard something that sounded like a switch, and then he heard the roar of the generator.

"I am back, all set. I have power now."

"You are a pretty remarkable woman, Jessica."

"Thanks, I don't see myself as remarkable. I see myself as self-sufficient."

"Now that you have power and you are back in the house. I will let you get back to work. So we can see each other sooner. Goodnight, Jessica. I love you."

"Goodnight, Timothy. I love you too."

Jessica was just about to go back into her darkroom when she heard her generator sputter and then go quiet. Then came the darkness. She turned her flashlight back on and made her way back outside to the generator. It had gas. She couldn't figure out why it had stopped. Until she went to hit the switch to start it again. It was then she realized the switch was off. She quickly turned it back on and scanned her surroundings. She couldn't see anyone or hear any movement.

Going back into the house, she went straight to her gun safe and took her pistol out. She loaded it and walked back out onto the porch. Scanning the perimeter of the woods, she still couldn't see or hear anyone. She took the safety off her gun, pulled back the slide, and fired a round into the darkness.

"That's a warning shot! I am armed, willing, and able to protect myself! I don't know who you are or why you are playing games. Leave me alone or you will face the consequences."

She walked back into the house, locked all her doors, and went back to work. The thought crossed her mind to call Timothy back and tell him someone had shut down her generator, but she decided that would just cause him to worry. She brought her pistol with her wherever she went in the house for the rest of the night. Even when she went to bed, it was within her reach, in case she needed it.

Jessica was glad her dad had taught her how to use a gun at an early age. She knew she shouldn't have fired the shot into the darkness. It was reckless of her to do so. She never felt as vulnerable as she did earlier though when she realized someone had turned off her generator. It was a feeling she wasn't familiar with and she didn't like feeling that way. Firing the shot gave her control over the situation. It had enabled her to take her power back.

Thinking about her dad got her thinking about her biological parents. She had names, and she had faces. Sadly, her biological father had died when she was about two years old. Her mother, though, as far as anyone knew, was still alive. She would do some research on the genealogy website in the morning. She had her name. It was a start. Jessica drifted off to sleep.

The next morning, Jimmy was making his morning rounds on the ATV around the island. He saw nothing out of the ordinary. The rickety ferry boat was just docking, and he recognized Samuel's truck. He must have had to go onto the mainland to get parts, Jimmy thought to himself. Samuel was always fixing something around the island, so it wasn't unusual for him to go back and forth to the mainland.

Jimmy hadn't slept well the night before. He felt bad about not believing Jessica at first and for suspecting Timothy of taking advantage of the situation. He could not think of anyone on the island with the motive to hurt either Jessica or Alexandria. An outsider getting on the island was nearly impossible as well. None of it made sense to him. He was missing something, but he didn't know what.

Timothy woke up and got straight to work on his article again. He hadn't been able to really get much done after his phone call with Jessica. He just couldn't get her out of his mind. It was difficult for him to not call her. She was right, though. They needed to focus on their work first, then they could meet up again. Just the thought of holding her in his arms again drove him crazy.

Awakening to the sputtering of her generator again, Jessica bolted upright and reached for her pistol. Realizing it was daytime already made her relax a bit because that meant the generator was most likely out of gas. She got dressed, made sure she had her pistol, and went outside to check on the generator.

It indeed had run out of gas. Before refilling it, she flipped the transfer switch to see if they had restored the power. Thankfully, it had been. She looked around to see if there was any evidence of the person who shut off her generator. After three full walks around the house and finding nothing, she went inside to have breakfast.

Arthur awoke in his hotel room with the grim realization he was going to have a long day making notifications. He had gotten very little sleep the night before. The beeps and alarms that went off when Alexandria had gone into cardiac arrest had startled him from his nap the evening before. The scene that unfolded before him was something he would never forget. Nurses and doctors rushed into the room to revive her. Someone ushered him into the hallway. He still couldn't believe she was gone.

As Jessica opened up her laptop and typed in the genealogy website, she looked at the photos Mary had given her. She still couldn't believe she had spent time with her biological parents as a child. Of course, she was too young to actually remember, but the photographs were proof.

When she typed in Mira Kennedy, tons of information popped up. Now to narrow it down. She knew Mira was sixteen in 1992. That meant she would have been born in 1976. Jessica assumed Mira was born in Connecticut as well. A birth record for a Mira Kennedy popped up with a birth date of May 2, 1976. She saved it as a potential match. Next she found a marriage record for a Mira Kennedy to a Mathew Brockton in Cambridge, MA, October 5, 1994. Another maybe. She had leads. Cambridge wasn't that far. She could make a day trip and do some research, but first she needed to get her work done. She powered down her laptop and went to work downloading and editing her digital photographs on her computer in her studio.

Timothy felt good about getting the first draft written. He definitely felt he had extra motivation with this assignment. At the suggestion of Arthur, he requested to work with Jessica. He knew her photography work was top-notch and was a fan of her work, but he never expected to be attracted to her. A break was in order and he heated some leftover pizza and cracked open a beer.

Finishing his noontime ride around the island, Jimmy approached the rickety ferry dock and noticed the ferry incoming with Arthur's car on-board. He got a bad feeling in the pit of his stomach. Arthur had said he planned on staying close to Alexandria, especially until they found out who had pushed her. Him being on the ferry meant one of two things. Either the police figured out who had pushed her or she had taken a turn for the worse. His bet was on the latter of the two.

CHAPTER SIXTEEN

The move

MIRA WAS EXCITEDLY PACKING up her room into boxes. She had graduated the night before and would move into her new apartment within the next couple of days. Her parents still didn't like the fact she would live on her own. They felt she was too young, however; they knew their daughter was stubborn as a mule.

Mary had gone on strike and had locked herself in her room. She wasn't leaving her house and island. She was contesting the will and set out for a long, drawn-out fight for her share of the island. Stella and Betty resumed the routine they had used with Alexandria during her depression.

As for Alexandria, she had snapped back from her depths of despair and had moved back to her penthouse in the city. She left Mary to wallow in her misery. The business she and her husband had built needed her to be strong and take charge, so that is exactly what she did.

The days flew by till it was moving day. Mira packed boxes in her car and her dad helped the movers pack her furniture into the moving truck. They assured him he didn't need to help, but he insisted.

Mira's parents followed the moving truck while Mira followed behind them in her own car. She felt such a sense of adventure and freedom. Anything was possible in her mind. Her life was just beginning. She looked down at her left hand and smiled at the ring she had slipped on before driving.

Traffic was light, and they made it to her apartment in what seemed like no time at all. When Mira stepped out of the car, she stood there for a moment, looking up at the apartment building. She took a deep breath, slipped off the ring, put it in her pocket, and closed the door. The sounds of the city were invigorating to her. Cars honking, kids playing on the sidewalks, and taxi cabs driving by. The city was full of life and she felt alive with it.

The movers and her parents helped her get her things to her apartment. Her mom ran to the grocery store to stock her cabinets while her dad helped to rearrange the second hand living room furniture a half a dozen times until Mira decided she liked it the way they had first had it. Her parents were just about to leave when there was a knock on the apartment door.

When Mira answered the door, there was a man holding a pizza and a bottle of soda, smiling from ear to ear.

"Oh, we didn't order a pizza."

Mira said to the man as her parents peered over her shoulder.

"Indeed, you didn't. It is my welcome to the building gift. My name is Mathew Brockton and I live across the hall. I saw you moving in today and wanted to introduce myself and welcome you."

Mira's father ushered Mathew in and introduced himself and his wife. He let Mira do her own introductions. Mira thanked him for the pizza and offered for him to join them in eating it. Mathew declined the invitation, saying he didn't want to intrude, and that he had already eaten his dinner.

After Mathew had left, Mira and her parents sat and ate dinner together.

"Nice fellow there. Seems like quite the gentleman."

"I don't know. He seems so much older than Mira. I don't know how I feel about her living across the hall from a single man."

"Geez, Mom, he doesn't seem that much older than me. Besides, as dad said, he seemed very nice and gentlemanly."

They said their goodbyes after dinner and tears flowed down her mom's face. Mira couldn't believe the big deal her mom was making over leaving her until she remembered the last time she saw her own daughter. She hugged her mom tight and told her she would be fine.

Shortly after her parents left, she heard another knock on the door. When she opened it, there was Mathew standing there with a popped bag of microwave popcorn and a movie. She smiled and invited him in. She spent the first night in her first apartment on a first date with Mathew Brockton.

Coming out of her office, it surprised Alexandria to see Mr. Gilman and another man standing at her receptionist's desk.

"Mr. Gilman, did we have a meeting I forgot about?"

"No, Alexandria. I am turning over my practice to Arthur Brockton, my nephew. It's time for me to retire and enjoy life to the fullest."

Alexandria welcomed both men into her office, where she got to know her new lawyer. It was Arthur who brought up the workable compromise with Mary. Alexandria could let Mary live on the island in the manor house until she remarried or died. She agreed, except she added one clause. The clause stated that in the event Alexandria died and Mary was still unwed and living, she would have to vacate the island because it would revert over to the town as a nature preserve.

The phone call with her lawyer wasn't exactly what she expected, however Mary thought it was a suitable compromise. She took a walk down by the beach to think more about it and the ramifications. When she came back, she called her lawyer and said she would agree to the compromise.

Mira started work the Monday following her move. Mathew surprised her at her door when she got home and invited her over to his apartment for dinner. She accepted. The candlelight dinner he had prepared mesmerized her. They ate and talked about her first day. She told him how much she enjoyed her job and couldn't wait to start school in the fall. He talked about his business dealings and his plans for expansion.

After dinner, they watched another movie together. Mathew put his arm around her and she snuggled right into his chest. It was comforting to just curl up and watch a movie in his arms. She closed her eyes and breathed in his cologne. She felt the rise of desire building inside her. When she opened her eyes and looked up at him, he was looking back at her with the same intense desire flickering in his eyes. He gently lifted her chin and kissed her lips ever so softly. She responded with more intensity than she had expected, and soon he carried her to his bed.

Mathew and Mira settled into a nightly routine of dinner, a movie, and passionate lovemaking. Soon they started discussing moving in together. They knew they had to tell her parents about their relationship before they took that step, though. They planned a trip home to Mira's parents for Labor Day Weekend.

Classes were starting the week before, so the quick break would help ease her back into school. Her parents were excited to see her. They hadn't been able to make a visit up yet because of their busy schedules. When she said she would bring her boyfriend home also to meet them, there was silence at first on the other end of the line. She assured them they would love him as much as she did.

"Love. Did you just say you loved a man you have only known for six weeks?"

"Yes, Mom, I did. I feel like I have known him for years, though. Everything just comes naturally with him."

Mira was smiling when she got off the phone with her.

Labor Day weekend came and Mathew turned on the charm to win Mira's parents over. It wasn't hard with her dad. Her mom was not comfortable with the age difference at all. Her husband kindly reminded her there was a ten-year difference between her and him and their relationship was great. By the end of the weekend, Mathew had asked her parents for their blessing in asking Mira to marry him, which they gave, and then Mira told them of their plans to move in together.

They set their wedding date as October 5th. Mira was looking through bridal magazines when nausea overcame her. She barely made it to the bathroom when her lunch decided it wasn't staying down. Mathew came home to find her hugging the toilet bowl. He rubbed her back and held her hair.

When he asked her if there was anything he could get her, she simply looked at him.

"A pregnancy test."

Mathew happily went down to the drugstore and got the item she requested. He also stocked up on ginger ale and saltine crackers. He had heard that helped to ease morning sickness in pregnant women.

Mira brushed her teeth to get the taste of vomit out of her mouth as she waited for the results of the pregnancy test. Two minutes later, Mathew was lifting her up in his arms and swinging her around. She protested mildly because it made her queasy. They were both extremely happy they would get married and start a family all at once. Mira suggested they hold off from telling anyone about the pregnancy until after the wedding, though. She didn't want any wrinkles in her day. She knew she wouldn't be showing, so it wasn't a big issue not telling anyone.

The wedding was a small gathering of mostly Mira's family and Mathew's business associates. She insisted that the wedding venue have a gazebo and that the ceremony would occur there, much to the dismay of her mother, who wanted her to have a more traditional church wedding. They decided they would wait until her semester was over before they went on their honeymoon.

At Christmas time they sprung the news of the baby on her parents. They had excitement and concern. They were afraid she was going to throw her education away. She assured them, as did Mathew, that her education would continue and she would still keep her job until she had to take maternity leave.

On May 2, 1995, on her nineteenth birthday, Mira gave birth to a healthy 6lb 6oz baby boy. She insisted on naming him Richard Mathew Brockton. She was so happy the day they left the hospital together. The sadness she felt knowing she had missed that with her daughter passed as she stared down at her perfect baby boy sleeping in her arms.

Her daughter would turn three soon. It had been almost a year since she saw her. She yearned for that contact. She had the address of the Greenhalls and she sent a birthday card to her daughter anonymously. It made her feel better knowing she was doing what she could to keep that connection open, hopefully.

On June seventh, she baked a cake and sang happy birthday to her daughter while tears streamed down her face. Mathew sang with her and hugged her tight. Little Richard was already a month old and was growing like a weed. He was 12 lbs.5oz. She cherished the time she had with him and relished in each milestone, no matter how tiny. She had missed all of that with her daughter, and she would not miss them with her son.

She found a home daycare close by that had room for Richard when it was time for her to go back to work. It was very hard saying goodbye on the first day. As she got back into the swing of things at work and when school started back up, it got easier to leave Richard in the competent hands of the daycare provider.

Mira was happy with her life. She had a loving husband and a beautiful son. There was nothing more she could ask for, except more kids. She loved being a mom. Mathew convinced her they should wait until Richard was at least a year old before they should have another child. He was concerned it would be too much for her with school, work, and being a mom. Mira, though, seemed to thrive with the challenges of her crazy schedule. She made the dean's list every semester and received a promotion as the senior partner's secretary.

CHAPTER SEVENTEEN

Bad news

JIMMY WAITED AT THE ferry dock for Arthur to drive his car off. When he drove up, he saw the grief written all over his face. Arthur and Alexandria were more than just lawyer and client. Over the years, they had become companions. Not lovers though, Alexandria could not open her heart up to any potential love interests after losing her whole family in one day. Arthur had fallen deeply in love with Alexandria and was content to just be her confidant and companion for all these years. Jimmy felt bad for him, his pain must have been unbearable.

Arthur and Alexandria had hit it off immediately when he had taken over for his uncle's law practice. They both had lost their spouses and children in tragic accidents. Arthur's had perished in a house fire two years before Alexandria's family had lost their lives in the sailing accident. Their losses brought them together, since each could relate to what the other had gone through. Together, they were a force to be reckoned with in any of Alexandria's business dealings.

As Arthur pulled his car off the ferry, he drove right up to Jimmy, standing by his ATV. Getting out of the car, he was visibly distraught and Jimmy could tell he had been crying. Jimmy pulled Arthur to him in a big bear hug, and as Arthur hugged him back, he sobbed uncontrollably.

Regaining his composure, Arthur pulled away and wiped the tears from his face.

"I am sorry. I don't know what came over me and I don't know why I am blubbering like an idiot."

"No apologies necessary. Arthur. You loved her. It's a tough loss for all here on the island, however, it's much greater for you,"

"Thank you for understanding. Now, speaking of those on the island. They need to come to the manor house immediately. I need to tell them all together. I need to assure them Alexandria had changed her will and they all will continue to have jobs and their houses here on the island."

"Yes, sir!"

Jimmy climbed onto his ATV to fulfill Arthur's request.

Arthur took a deep breath and climbed back into his car. He drove to the manor house where he would be the one to tell everyone of Alexandria's death. He would tell Mary before the others, so she had some time to process the news before she had to face all the employees on the island. Phone calls had to be made as well.

Timothy heard his cell phone ringing. It was surprising to see Arthur was calling him. He hit the green button.

"Hello Arthur, how is Alexandria doing? Good news, I Hope."

"Good afternoon, Timothy. I am afraid it is not good news. Alexandria had a heart attack last night. They could not revive her."

Arthur tried to hold his composure.

"Oh, Arthur, I am so sorry to hear that. She seemed to be such a nice person. Is there anything I can do?"

"Thank you. Yes, she was a wonderful woman. I will miss her dearly. There is something you can do. Could you please let Jessica know? I think she might take it better coming from you. Poor kid, just finds some family, and in an instant, one member is gone."

"Sure thing Arthur. I will call her as soon as we get off the phone. You take care, and if you need anything else, please call and ask."

"Thank you. I will let you know as soon as we make the funeral arrangements."

The two men hung up the phone. Timothy had no problem calling Jessica. He was dying to talk to her again, anyway. Although he had resigned himself to trying to wait, this gave him the perfect excuse to hear her sweet voice again.

Jessica was working on some digital editing when her cell phone rang. She picked it up and smiled when she recognized it was Timothy. Ironically, the pictures she had been editing were the ones she had snuck of him writing.

"Hey, we will never get to see each other in person if we keep taking breaks and talking on the phone."

"I know, I know. But I had to call you. I just got off the phone with Arthur. He asked me to call you."

This was going to be harder than he thought. He really wished he could tell her in person. He wished he could hold her and comfort her. This long distance stuff sucked.

"Wait, Arthur asked you to call me? Please do not tell me something bad has happened to Alexandria."

Jessica's stomach knotted up. Tears welled up in her eyes in anticipation of potential bad news.

"I am so, so sorry, Jessica. My wish is I could be there right now with you. I hate having to tell you this over the phone. Alexandria had a heart attack last night. I am truly sorry. Do you want me to come there? I can take the next ferry across and be there in no time. I can finish the article there."

Timothy's words rambled. He felt so awkward telling her like this. All he could hear on the other end of the phone were quiet sobs.

"Jessica, Jess, are you okay? I am so sorry. Please say something."

"I am here. Please come, I need you, Timothy."

Jessica could barely choke out the words. She felt lost. Life was just too cruel, and it felt as though every time things seemed to look up, fate pulled the rug right out from under her. She barely knew Alexandria, however she had felt that kindred spirit with her from the beginning and then learning she was family. Real biological family, it was hard. Gaining family and losing them all in a matter of days. Timothy would be there that night. He would hold her in his arms and comfort her. That was unquestionably a comforting thought.

Timothy hung up the phone after assuring Jessica he would be there that evening. His packing was done, and he was ready to go in less than a half hour. Getting a reservation on the next ferry wasn't as easy. He drove to the ferry terminal and waited in the stand by lane, hoping to get on the next available ferry.

In the parlor of the manor house, the residents and employees of the island had gathered at the request of Arthur. Mary sat composed on the sofa. Jimmy was standing, making sure everyone was present. He was observing them all. Everyone in this room was a suspect in the murder of Alexandria in his mind. He noticed Samuel was missing and took Arthur aside to tell him he wasn't there. Arthur told him he had already informed him. He had seen him getting off the rickety ferry as he was waiting to get on. Samuel had said he had parts to get.

"I am sure you are all wondering why I have called you all together. You are all aware our beloved Ms. Alexandria had a dreadful accident the other day. I am deeply saddened to tell you all that last night she suffered a major heart attack. Our beloved Alexandria is at peace now with her loving family."

There were audible gasps around the room. Many employees, including Stella and Betty, wept openly. Someone made a statement.

"What does that mean for us?"

Arthur continued.

"I know that everyone here knew that Alexandria had planned on bequeathing the island to the town and having it turned into a nature preserve when she passed. Recently, she changed her mind. The reading of the Will will take place after her funeral. I assure you, no one will leave the island. The new owners have already stated they want things to remain exactly the way they are."

They heard a collective sigh of relief around the room, along with murmurings of who the new owners would be. Considering as far as they all knew, there were no living heirs, they were all thoroughly confused. Arthur guaranteed they would all find out who the new owners would be after the funeral. Then he set tasks to be done to complete the arrangements.

Timothy boarded the four o'clock ferry at Orient Point, heading to New London. He was eager to get to Jessica's house to comfort her. He knew he had a two-hour ride across the Long Island Sound, so he set up his laptop and started working on his article.

Mid way through the trip, his work immersed him, and another passenger losing his footing and bumping into it rattled his table.

"Sorry, man, I didn't mean to bump into the table like that. Guess my sea legs aren't as good as they used to be."

As Timothy looked up to acknowledge the gentleman, it surprised him to recognize him as the grumpy Samuel from Gardiners Island. The one that had shown him and Jessica to the Osprey nests.

"No problem, hey aren't you Samuel? You took me and my photographer friend out to the osprey nests on Gardiners Island."

"Yeah, that's me. Where's your photographer friend?"

"I am actually going to see her. What brings you out this way?"

"Oh, she lives out this way? I am on a hunt. For tractor parts that are scarce. Hoping to get lucky and find them in Connecticut."

"Yeah, she is from Connecticut. Good luck with the parts search. Oh, sorry about the loss of Alexandria."

"Thanks."

Was all Samuel responded with as he swayed while walking away.

Jessica couldn't concentrate on her work. The sadness she felt at the loss of Alexandria was too much for her to bear. She knew it would be a few hours before Timothy would be there. So she went for a ride through her trails on her ATV. Riding always seemed to clear her mind and her heart because it brought her out into nature, where she felt most at peace. She rode to one of her favorite spots.

A downed tree ripped from the earth from one of the many storms that had gone through her town in the past. It sat precariously parallel to the ground. She pulled herself up onto it at the base where the roots were showing and climbed up on it. Walking as if on a balance beam slowly, she walked the slight incline of the trunk to sit where she could nestle herself between some branches. It wasn't very high off the ground, maybe eight feet. However, the view of the nearby meadow from her spot was always breathtaking and calming. Many times she had sat in this very spot and witnessed does grazing as their fawns frolicked.

As she sat perched in the tree, she leaned back against the branch and closed her eyes. They snapped open when she remembered she would now inherit the island and Alexandria's business, along with Jimmy. She knew nothing about real estate, especially in a big city like New York. How the heck was she going to manage that? She was sure Jimmy had no clue either and figured he would feel more comfortable handling the island. Thinking about having to take over Alexandria's business, Jessica realized she needed to finish up her last assignment. She climbed down from the tree and rode back to the house to get back to work.

Timothy had finished the final draft of his article while he was on the ferry. He was happy to complete his portion of the assignment so that he could focus his energy on helping Jessica through the loss of Alexandria. As he descended the steps of the ferry to get into his car, his thoughts went to the night they had found out there was no possibility of them being relatives. Making love to Jessica that night was amazing. He was still shocked to find out that was her first time. He understood her reasoning, about not getting into a physical relationship with being adopted and all, however he had had a few drunken encounters over the years where he gave in to his primal desires. Holding Jessica in his arms again was the only thing he desired at that moment in time.

As he drove off the ferry and across the train tracks, he heard a thump, thump, and soon realized he had a flat tire. Pulling over to the side of the road, he put the car in park and cautiously got out of his car to check the tire. Yup, it was flat, and he didn't have a spare. He called AAA, and it frustrated him to find out it would be at least a half hour.

Timothy called Jessica to tell her there was a delay. She offered to come help, and he refused, saying she could use that extra time to get the pictures ready for the assignment. In the end, she agreed and got back to work.

Jessica finished picking the photographs she was going to submit with Timothy's article within forty-five minutes of Timothy's call. She was happy she stayed and finished her work. Knowing it would be another half hour before Timothy would pull into her driveway, she went to go sit out on her porch swing to wait. As she opened her door, she found an envelope on the front steps. She had heard no car drive up her driveway. And heard no one go onto her porch. She opened the envelope and found a typed note.

If you return to Gardiners Island, you will never leave. Don't go back.

CHAPTER EIGHTEEN

Lena's wedding

THREE YEARS HAD FLOWN by since the tragedy that had taken six lives. Life had moved on for those most affected. Mary was an exception. She became almost a recluse, staying on the island and rarely going to the mainland. No more trips into the city, or Broadway shows. She received many invitations to all the Hampton elite gatherings. She declined every single one. The island became her sanctuary and her life. She no longer hosted the summer gathering either and tightened up access to the island by outsiders. The last time anyone from the public without ties to the island was on the island was for the memorial service.

As Mary rummaged through her mail and sorted the invitations that had come in for various events, she came across one from her cousin Rita, inviting her to her daughter Lena's wedding.

You are cordially invited
To witness the nuptials
Of
Lena Duvall
Daughter of
Rita and Thomas Duvall
Of East Hampton, NY
To
Steven Weston
Son of
Peter and Cynthia Weston
Of East Hampton, NY
On
Saturday July 5th, 1997
At
2 O'clock in the afternoon
At

Triune Baptist Church
33 Eastville Ave
Sag Harbor, New York
Reception immediately following at
The Hedges Inn
74 James Lane
East Hampton, NY

When they were younger, Rita and Mary had been close. They were almost like sisters instead of cousins. Rita was 6 years older and had been the rebellious one in the family, leading to an unplanned pregnancy at 15. Lena had been the child born out of wedlock and Mary had babysat her frequently for Rita.

Rita was supposed to give Lena up for adoption. However, after seeing her precious baby alone in the nursery, she changed her mind. It had been a hard path. Rita had navigated single parent life well and had successfully attended Community College getting a paralegal degree.

Mary reminisced about those times. It was the summer before she went off to college that their friendship and closeness ended. They had both attended the annual Gardiner summer kickoff party on Gardiners Island. Alexandria's parents hosted. They were rarely home, except for their traditional parties.

Both girls had a big crush on Richard Gardiner, as did most of the debutantes from the Hamptons. His icy blue eyes mesmerized them all. They had agreed, a pinky promise though, that neither would pursue him out of consideration of the other's feelings.

Mary broke that pact the night of the party. They had all gone down to the beach and started a bonfire. Richard started flirting with Mary, and Mary flirted back. By the end of the night, they were the latest couple of the Hamptons and Rita hardly ever spoke to Mary again. The invitation to Lena's wedding was purely out of obligation.

She almost tossed it in the trash when she remembered Lena had attended St. Catherine's school. The same school where the photograph of Richard's mistress was from, Mira. *Could they have been friends?* She needed an escort. She couldn't go alone and knew exactly who she would take. He owed her.

She had hired Samuel to be the island mechanic and handyman about a year after Richard's death. Mary felt sorry for him. He had suffered burns on his hands and face in some accident that he rarely would speak about. She gave him the job on the island and he fixed up one of the old servant's cabins for himself to live in. She also paid for cosmetic surgery to help with the scarring of his face. He owed her. Even with the scars, he was a handsome man, so that was another bonus for her taking him to the wedding. He would serve a purpose as an air of mystery, which was perfect for her return to the Hampton social scene.

Mira was excited to see Lena again. She had come to East Hampton for the bridal shower and her last fitting for her Matron of Honor's dress. The last time she had been in the area was for the memorial service. The thought of that day brought back a flood of emotions. She said goodbye to Richard and her daughter that day. Wiping away the tear that fell down her cheek, she turned into the driveway of her friend's beach house. Holding onto the wonderful memories would always help her get through the bad ones.

The two women hugged in the driveway and Lena took her friend's hand as they walked up the steps and onto the wrap around veranda. Around back Rita was sitting sipping lemonade almost exactly as she had the first time Mira had met her. The three women sat and caught up on all the latest news in each others lives all afternoon.

In the morning, Lena and Mira met the other bridesmaids at the dress shop for their final fittings. Mira, being four months pregnant and showing, was stunned that her dress was getting tight and wasn't zipping up all the way. She burst into tears. The seamstress, working on her dress, handed her some tissues and reassured her she could fix the dress so it would zip and wouldn't be too tight.

That evening, the bridal party took Lena out on the town for her bachelorette party. Since Mira was pregnant, she was a designated driver. The women showered their friend with drinks and helped her celebrate the next milestone in her life.

Thankfully, the bridal shower for the next day was in the late afternoon, so those that had partaken in too much alcohol had time to recover. Mira, who had not drank was up early getting the final touches finished on her friend's bridal shower. She smiled as she remembered her own wedding three years ago and how Lena had been her Maid Of Honor.

Sure, her wedding had been small and occurred rather quickly, to the dismay of many friends and family. However, it was a beautiful day that she would cherish forever. She and Mathew were happy. They had built a significant life for themselves in the last three years. They were expecting their second child. Mira was still doing great in school, working towards her law degree, and they had promoted her to a paralegal at the law firm she worked at.

The bridal shower went on without a hitch. Rita fawned over Lena and all the fabulous gifts she received. It would set Lena and Steven to start their new life together in their new home, thanks to the generosity of their guests. One invited guest who didn't show up was Mary. She hadn't sent a gift either.

Mary had thrown the invitation to the bridal shower in the trash. She hadn't even RSVP'd to it. She was planning on making a grand entrance at the wedding. Waiting till the last minute to even respond to the wedding invitation. She was glad that the RSVP date was after the bridal shower. It helped to make her attendance at the wedding more of a surprise.

The day of the wedding arrived and Mary walked into the church, accompanied by Samuel. As one groomsman ushered her down the aisle to her seat, she was fully aware of the turning of heads and the whispers behind hands. She smiled calmly as she took her seat, and Samuel slid into the pew alongside her. The reactions were exactly what she expected, and had wanted. The rush she got from the attention made her feel alive.

She perused the program that was handed to her, listing the names of the bridal party, what readings would take place, and the hymns that they would sing. As she did, the name she was looking for jumped out at her. Mira, Mira Brockton, listed as Matron of Honor. She couldn't wait to see the bridal party walk down the aisle so she could verify it was the same girl from the picture. Then she noticed another name that enraged her. Richard, Richard Brockton listed as the ring bearer. It had to be her, Richard's mistress. Had she been pregnant when he passed away?

The processional music started and the wedding party started down the aisle as the Groom and his Best Man stood waiting at the altar for his bride. As Mira walked down the aisle holding her son's hand, she smiled at all the guests. Then, as she passed Mary, they briefly locked eyes, and Mira felt a cold shiver run down her back. The look on Mary's face was one of recognition that filled Mira with confusion.

Her mother Rita and her father Thomas escorted Lena down the aisle. Mary smiled and gave a small little wave as Rita caught her glance. Rita smiled back, although she was seething underneath the fake smile. She couldn't believe Mary had the audacity to actually show.

After the ceremony, the bridal party lined up outside the church so that guests could congratulate the newlyweds. As Mary made her way down the line with Samuel, Rita watched her. The mystery man that was with her cousin intrigued Rita. He was tall, bald and had grey eyes. He had some scarring on his face and hands, yet it didn't diminish his appearance in the least. She found him quite alluring.

Mary got to Mira in the reception line and leaned in, and whispered in her ear.

"I know who you are. You whore."

Then continued down the line to congratulate her cousin's daughter on her marriage.

Mira was a bit stunned, yet she kept her composure after what Mary had said. Smiling and greeting all the guests while gripping her restless two-year-old's hand. She wouldn't let anyone ruin her best friend's wedding and she certainly would not engage her ex-lover's widow in any drama.

At the reception, after a few glasses of wine, Rita got the courage to interrupt Mary and Samuel dancing and asked if she could cut in.

"I pinky promise it's just for one dance."

She said to Mary as Samuel took her hand and started the next slow dance with her.

Mary understood the reference and went back to her table, annoyed at both Rita and Samuel. Why Samuel was obliging her cousin's whim perplexed her. Whose side was he on, anyway? She drank some wine as she loathingly watched Samuel and Rita enjoying their dance together. Then she noticed Mira dancing with whom she presumed was her husband. As she watched them, she couldn't help but feel like she knew him. He seemed very familiar with his jet-black hair and his mannerisms.

She finally remembered where she had seen him before. It was at the memorial service! When the dance ended, she walked up to the man and introduced herself.

"Good afternoon, my name is Mary Gardiner. My husband was Richard Gardiner. I believe you attended his memorial service three years ago."

"Why yes, I am so sorry for your loss. Richard had been a business associate. He was a good man. Great golfer too. We played several times together."

"Thank you. And your name is?"

"Oh, I am sorry. I forgot my manners. Mathew Brockton and this is my lovely wife, Mira and our son Richard."

"We met in the reception line. Your son is adorable. So, how did you two lovebirds meet?"

Mathew indulged Mary in the story of how he and Mira had met after she moved into his apartment building. Soon Mary became bored with the conversation and looked for Samuel. She found him standing at the bar, engaged in what looked like a flirtatious conversation with Rita. As she walked up, Rita edged closer to Samuel and placed a hand on his chest as she was laughing.

Mary, recognizing what Rita was trying to do, walked up to Samuel and grabbed his hand.

"There you are, dear. I have been looking all over for you. I think I am ready to go home and make this a private party for two."

Samuel smiled and shifted his body toward Mary, causing Rita's hand to drop from his chest.

"Dear, that sounds like an amazing idea."

They said their obligatory goodbyes and headed back to the manor house and Gardiner Island. Mary felt she had made her presence known and once again felt more alive than she had in the last three years.

Mira felt sick to her stomach. It wasn't pregnancy sickness either. The words Mary had whispered in her ear ran through her mind. The fact she approached Mathew and recognized him being at the memorial service made her stomach do even more flips. She told Lena she wasn't feeling well, and they left the reception a little early and headed to their hotel room to get some rest. They would head home in the morning.

CHAPTER NINETEEN

Reunited

As Timothy drove up the driveway of Jessica's house, he understood why she loved the solitude of her surroundings. He thought that where he lived in Riverhead was rural, especially compared to the city, but seeing where Jessica lived, he realized he was wrong. This was rural.

Jessica sat on her porch swing, waiting for Timothy. She was debating whether she should show him the note she received or tell him about the generator issue. This wasn't the first time she had dealt with a stalker. After the Amazon pictures had earned her awards and more notoriety, she periodically dealt with these types of situations. This time it was a little more unnerving, though, with the incidents that had occurred while she was on Gardiners Island. They could be coincidences or they could be connections. She didn't know what to think.

The note mentioned Gardiners Island, however stalkers have mentioned places she had been on assignment before. She let it all go and would not tell Timothy about it. Her focus needed to be on grieving Alexandria's death and preparing herself to help run Alexandria's business.

The sound of Timothy's car startled her out of her thoughts. Calmness enveloped her as she realized it was him. The thought of being able to hug him again brought a smile to her face. As she put her foot down to stop the swing, Timothy's car came to a stop.

Timothy hopped out of his car and made quick work of the steps of the porch. Jessica had barely stood up when she found herself wrapped in his powerful arms. She felt safe with him, a feeling she hadn't noticed she didn't feel until she met him.

Tears came quickly for Jessica, and Timothy let her get them out. He knew she needed to grieve. She would grieve more than just Alexandria. She would also grieve the lost family connection that she had just made and also her former life. Taking over Alexandria's business would be a huge undertaking.

She regained her composure and showed Timothy her home. When they got to her studio room, she showed him the photographs to go with the article. He agreed they were the perfect pictures.

They read and edited his article, added the pictures, and sent the assignment off to the editors at National Geographic. With the assignment finally done, they turned their attention to their budding relationship. They went on an actual date.

With Timothy not knowing the area, he let Jessica plan their date. She took him to The Harp and Dragon Pub for dinner and planned on taking a walk down at the Norwich Marina afterward.

She drove her car and was lucky to find a parking spot out front. Jessica watched Timothy's reaction to the little city atmosphere. She could see the amazement that within a matter of minutes, they went from a very rural area to this mini city. It still differed from the big city hustle and bustle of New York City. They sat at a high top table for two.

Timothy was aware of Jessica watching him. He loved how she smiled at his reactions. It definitely amazed him at how diverse the region was that she lived in. Jessica seemed to know several of the regulars in the pub as they waved or shouted hello to her. Timothy felt a brief pang of jealousy when he realized that most of them were men.

The waitress came over to get their order. They ordered a couple of beers, pretzel bites, and cheesesteak sliders to start. Their conversation flowed so easily from one subject to another. Jessica reflected on how easy this all seemed with Timothy. She had never had this type of relationship and she was really liking it a lot.

They both ordered the prime rib special for dinner. The tenderness of the meat blew Timothy away. The fact Jessica could finish the king sized meal was astonishing. She laughed at his astonishment and teased him he must be used to some prim and proper model types.

As they left the pub, they held hands and walked to the marina, where there was a gentleman with a telescope set up to view the stars. They paid the man ten dollars to look through the telescope. The clarity of the stars they could view fascinated them. As they continued to walk around the marina, the air got chilly and Jessica visibly got cold. Timothy put his arm around her to warm her up. They headed back to her house.

Back home, Jessica made Timothy a cup of coffee and herself a cup of tea. They sat and watched a Netflix movie and warmed up. Timothy put his coffee cup down, took Jessica's cup out of her hands, and gently pulled her towards him. He kissed her passionately with all his pent up lust for her over the last few days. He felt as if he was going to explode.

Jessica's response to his kiss was just as explosive. She felt the rush through her body. The hunger to have him hold her skin to skin. To feel his heartbeat against hers. The desire to feel as though they were one. She took his hands and led him to her bedroom, where they fulfilled each other's desires all throughout the night.

In the morning, Jessica awoke nestled in Timothy's arms. A strong feeling of contentment overcame her it actually brought tears to her eyes. Feeling a teardrop falling on his arm alarmed Timothy that he had done something wrong.

"Jessica, are you okay?"

"I am fine. Actually, more than fine, I am absolutely wonderful."

Jessica wiped the tears and rolled in his arms to face him.

"Then why are you crying?"

"They are happy tears. I have never felt more happy and content in my life. As I do, right now, right here, in your arms."

Timothy held her tighter and kissed her gently on her forehead.

Timothy's cell phone ringing startled them out of their embrace. When he grabbed it and answered it, Jessica rolled out of bed and put a bathrobe on.

"Good morning Timothy, it's Arthur. I just wanted to update you on the funeral arrangements for Alexandria."

The two men conversed, and Arthur told Timothy Saturday morning on Gardiners Island they would hold the funeral. And they would do the reading of the will on Saturday evening. Arthur also expressed that Mary had said they were more than welcome to stay at the manor house for the weekend. Timothy told Arthur he would give the information to Jessica and they would let them know their decision on where they would stay before they came.

Jessica bristled at the thought of going back to the island and staying in the manor house. She resigned herself to staying there one night. They agreed they would get a room at an area bed-and-breakfast for Friday night and Sunday night. She almost brought up the note and the generator issue, however, she kept that to herself, for now.

Timothy didn't like the thought of going back to the island and staying at the manor house, either.

It was still unsettling about Jessica's near drowning and ATV accident. He knew he was going to be by her side the whole time because he wanted nothing to happen to her. He couldn't help but feel she was feeling uneasy too, even as she was trying to reassure him that everything would be okay.

Jessica took Timothy on a tour of her property on her ATVs. She showed him the tree and the meadow. The realization that she was opening up a part of herself she had never opened up to anyone else hit him. They spent the whole day just enjoying each other's company. Timothy fell just as much in love with Jessica's property as he had fallen in love with her. Jessica was falling in love with Timothy, fast and hard.

The young couple spent the next few days exploring various sites together. Each time Jessica brought Timothy to a new place, he fell in love with her more. He loved how she enjoyed the outdoors and couldn't believe the amount of places she took him hiking. It was when she took him to Mohegan Sun Casino and they bar hopped he realized just how diverse a woman Jessica was. She could have fun anywhere.

Time seemed to travel so fast when they were together. Soon they packed Timothy's car to head to Gardiners Island for the funeral. Timothy tried to keep conversations light to help ease Jessica's anxiety about the will and her inheritance. Spending time with Timothy had all but erased any of Jessica's concerns for her own safety, and she concluded in her mind that her stalker had probably moved on, as was usually the case.

They made it to Long Island and took the scenic ride to East Hampton where they were staying at a bed-and-breakfast for the night. After checking in, they went to the small café they had originally met at to have dinner. When they walked in, Jessica noticed a large party sitting in the back corner.

She recognized two of the women as the two that had been in the corner watching her the first time. She also recognized the young woman who had waited on her for the first time in this café. The others facing her she didn't recognize, however; she assumed the men sitting next to each

woman were their husbands. There were five people with their backs to her. A man with black hair,
a woman with long curly red hair, a young adult
male with strawberry blonde hair, a young adult
woman with long curly red hair, and a teenage
boy with strawberry blonde hair. They gave her
the impression of a family and she felt a pang of
longing, which led to feelings of grief.

It wasn't until they all got up to leave that
she could see their faces. As she recognized the
woman walking out the door as an older version
of the young woman in the photo Mary had given
her, she dropped her fork to her plate. Her stomach did flips, and it paralyzed her with excitement
and fear. Jessica realized she missed her chance
as the family climbed into their car and drove
away outside of the café.

"Are you okay?"

"Yeah, did you see how much that woman re-
sembled the picture Mary had given me of my
mother?"

"Yes, I also noticed the resemblance to you of the younger woman, who I presume was her daughter, possibly your half-sister."

"Why didn't I get up and ask her who she was?"

"You were afraid of rejection? Afraid she wanted nothing to do with you after all these years. Afraid her family wouldn't accept you either."

"Maybe. I just froze."

"Maybe we can track her down. She is obviously in the area."

"Yeah, maybe we can."

Jessica and Timothy finished their dinner and drove back to the bed-and-breakfast they were staying at. They had become all too familiar with sharing a bed and drifted off to sleep, discussing the possibilities of moving in together.

CHAPTER TWENTY

Going home

MIRA STARTED THE POT of coffee and retrieved the morning paper off the front step as she had for the last 20 years. Picking up the paper, as she closed the door to the suburban neighborhood they had settled in, she opened the paper to the business section. It had been her morning ritual for as long as she could remember, opening to the business section and putting the paper next to Mathew's breakfast plate for him to read when he came down.

As she opened the paper, she met with the headline, *CEO, and President of Cromwell Realty and Investments Group, Alexandria Cromwell Dies After*

Tragic Fall. Her hand covered her mouth as she sat down to read the rest of the article. The tears fell. She knew this day would come at some point in their lives. She just never expected it to be this soon.

Mathew came downstairs, fixing his tie. As he walked into the dining room and found his wife crying. He rushed to her to find out what had upset her. All she could do was point to the article. He sat down, put his head in his hands, and sobbed.

They both knew the death of Alexandria heralded a day of reckoning for them. They would finally reveal truths and they would hopefully learn to forgive themselves for their pasts. The funeral would be Saturday, and they made plans to attend. First, they had to sit down and explain everything to their three children.

Richard was their oldest. He was twenty-two years old and had just moved into his own apartment with a bunch of friends. He was working as an advertising executive for a social media company. Samantha was their middle child. She was twenty and was still going to college and working part time as a waitress. And then there was David, he was eighteen and fresh out of high school. With no job and no desire to even go to college.

Later that evening after dinner, Mira and Mathew sat their children down to tell them about their older sister and why they needed to attend the funeral of a woman, they had never met before. They were stunned at what they were told.

Richard was the first to react, and it wasn't what either of them was expecting. He got up silently, went to the door, and opened it. As he walked out the door, he looked back with contempt and disgust on his face while shaking his head. It was like a knife was driven straight into Mira's heart. She cried. Mathew put his arm around her and tried to soothe her.

Samantha sat there, not knowing what to say or think. All this time, she thought her family was perfect. Her mother was a successful lawyer. She had worked hard to get her own practice. To find out she had a child as an unwed teenager and had an affair with a married man was hard to wrap her head around. The only exciting part of all this was she had a sister! A big sister at that. Samantha had always wished for a sister and when David was born, she was very mad at her parents for weeks. How could her parents keep these secrets for so many years, though? They weren't the people that they portrayed to the outside world. Her dad held the darkest secrets, and that part scared her. She understood Richard's reaction.

David focused on the fact that the heirs to Alexandria's estate would inherit her real estate empire and Gardiners Island. He rushed to his room to google as much information as he could about the island and the business.

They all begrudgingly agreed to attend the funeral with their parents after a day or two of cooling off and processing the information they had. The only good part of the trip was they would stay with their mother's friend Lena, whom they all adored and called Aunt Lena. Although that was getting awkward for Richard as he was finding out he was having potent feelings for her daughter, Danielle. If they ever started a relationship, he would have to stop calling her mom Aunt Lena.

They all arrived at Lena and Steve's house in East Hampton on Thursday night. Lena cooked them a big pasta dinner and then they sat out on the deck overlooking their private beach with a view of the Atlantic ocean. Danielle and her two sisters, Erica and Stephanie, led Richard, Samantha, and David down to the beach where they could sit and enjoy time away from their parents.

Richard filled in Danielle and her sisters as to the news that his parents had told him and his siblings only a few short days prior. Their eyes bulged and their hands went over their mouths. Samantha gave Richard a glaring look. Danielle was the first to say something.

"I think I met your big sister two weeks ago. She was in the café I work at. I waited on her. My Mom and Grandma were in that day too and they told me later that they couldn't get over how much she looked like your Mom. And now that I think about it, she looks just like you, Samantha. She seemed really nice."

"What about everything else I said? Doesn't any of that bother you at all?"

"Secrets are big around here. Everybody has them, some bigger than others. Honestly, any secret that sticks it to Mary Gardiner is okay with me. She is the biggest bitch around."

"But.... what about the accident? What about the lies? Doesn't any of that sit wrong with you?"

"Well, yeah, but look where it all leads. You are sitting here with me."

Danielle smiled and stood up. She reached for Richard's hand and they took a walk down the shoreline as the waves crashed toward them.

The next night, they all went to dinner at the café Danielle worked at. When Jessica walked in with Timothy, Danielle immediately recognized her. She mentioned nothing because she didn't know how Richard would react. She assumed that her mother and grandmother either didn't recognize Jessica this time or they didn't want to say anything either.

It wasn't until they were all leaving that it appeared it startled Jessica to see her family for the first time. Danielle heard the fork crash against the plate. So did Richard, and at that moment, she saw recognition in his eyes. Danielle pushed him through the door and the two families got into their separate cars to head back to the house.

"She was in there!"

Richard looked back as they pulled away.

"Who was?"

"Jessica! Your daughter!"

"Really? Should we go back?"

"Yes!"

Richard, Samantha, and David were unified in their response.

"No. Tomorrow we will all meet her at the funeral. She will have too many questions that we can't answer until tomorrow."

Mira knew Mathew was right. They had to wait one more day. A silent tear rolled down her cheek. She had waited twenty-three years to see her daughter again. She prayed she would forgive her. Starting tomorrow, no more secrets and no more lies. Tomorrow, hopefully, they could start fresh, as a complete family.

The next morning, they all got ready to attend Alexandria's funeral. All the attendees were being shuttled over in vans to the island on the rickety old ferry. The shuttles started at 7 am and didn't stop until 10:30 am. Hundreds of friends, acquaintances, and business people came to pay their respects.

CHAPTER TWENTY-ONE

Alexandria's funeral

SLEEP WAS HARD FOR Jessica. She kept thinking about seeing her Mom and her potential siblings the night before. Her stomach had done flips all night long, and now she was downright nauseous. Alexandria's funeral was later in the morning, which added to the nervous stomach. She couldn't contain the nerves any longer and she bolted for the bathroom. Timothy awoke to the sounds of Jessica in the bathroom vomiting.

Timothy got out of bed and went to see if there was anything he could do to make Jessica feel any better. He rubbed her back and held her hair until she could stop, wishing there was more he could do. He didn't know how to help calm her nerves and he couldn't imagine all the thoughts running through her head at this moment.

They both showered, got dressed, and made their way downstairs to breakfast. Jessica picked at the scrambled eggs and bacon on her plate. Timothy encouraged her to at least eat the toast, which she got down.

After checking out, they headed to the island. Once on the island, Martin met them at the manor house, who showed them to their room for the night. Jessica was uneasy being back on the island and at the now creepy feeling house. Mary was a little friendlier, although she seemed on edge with all the hustle and bustle surrounding the funeral.

Jessica walked into the family cemetery where Alexandria's plot was dug and waited for her casket to be lowered into. The lighthouse monument that memorializes the six people who tragically lost their lives in the fatal sailing accident twenty-three years ago caught her eye. She was at that funeral with her adoptive parents, however;

she searched the recesses of her mind and could not remember being there. Her biological father, Richard Gardiner, had perished in that accident. She would never get the chance to know him.

There was a small headstone for the baby that Richard and Mary had lost. She knew the truth that he had survived birth and was then put up for adoption. She knew that the child had grown up on this island and would share in the inheritance along with her. Jessica had already decided to let Jimmy control the everyday workings of the island. She was hoping they could get past their rocky start and work together as cousins to manage Alexandria's estate.

As the morning dragged on, people filled the garden where chairs sat waiting for mourners to fill them. They lay Alexandria out in her casket for people to pay their respects. Arthur was up front, greeting the mourners and sharing stories about his beloved friend. The habitants of the island all mingled with the other mourners from the mainland. There was a buzz amongst the mourners wondering who the new owners of the island were and several were very blunt in asking the inhabitants. All the inhabitants could tell them was apparently Alexandria had left the island and the rest of her estate to someone, however they weren't aware of who yet.

Promptly at 11:00 am, the minister asked everyone to take a seat. Arthur, Mary, Jessica, Timothy, and Jimmy all sat in the front row reserved for family. The sight of Jessica, Timothy, and Jimmy sitting in the front row set off a buzz of whispers behind them from the attendees.

As the minister spoke of the spiritual journey that Alexandria's soul would now embark on. He reminded the mourners that a chapter in her journey had ended and a new one had started. He also mentioned she was now reunited with those she had lost two decades ago and that those in attendance should rejoice at her reunion. His message continued mentioning it was up to them all to continue her legacy and to remember her by sharing their personal experiences and stories of her with each other. He then invited attendees to come up and share any memories or stories with everyone.

Arthur was the first to step up and share.

"Good Morning, and thank you all for coming to pay your respects to Alexandria. As many of you know, I have been her family lawyer for many years. Over those years, we had developed a fond friendship. Although we were not romantically in-volved, I loved her more than anyone could ever understand. We met at a time we were both griev-ing the loss of our families. We found comfort in our shared tragedies. All will miss Alexandria, however, not nearly as much as by me."

As Arthur finished, he broke down in tears. He sat down next to Mary, who handed him some tissues. Several friends and business associates stepped up next. Each taking their time to explain their relationship to Alexandria and how much they already missed her. Some people told funny anecdotal stories of outings with Alexandria, and others spoke of her business prowess.

Mary, feeling a bit obligated to say something, finally stepped up in front of everyone.

"It is no secret that there was no love lost between Alexandria and myself. However, I will forever be grateful to her for allowing me to continue living here after the death of my beloved husband. Losing him was the greatest loss I ever had to bear and losing my home also would have been even more unbearable."

Jessica didn't know what compelled her to get up next when Mary sat down. However, she got up to the small podium and looked out at all the mourners gathered to say goodbye to her cousin, whom she had just met. She didn't know what she was going to say, and as she stood there, the nervousness of her stomach returned. Then she looked out into the mourners and she was stunned to see her mother and her family sitting there. And she spoke.

"Good morning all. My name is Jessica Greenhall. Some of you might know me as an award-winning photographer. And you are probably wondering what I am doing here. Two weeks ago I had an assignment here on Gardiners Island. Before stepping foot onto the island, I had felt a connection with Alexandria. You see, we both have lost loved ones to tragedies. I won't go into details of my life because we are here to honor and remember Alexandria's life. I had the pleasure of meeting her while I was here on the island. That meeting solidified that connection. One of the last things she did while with us was to help me find out who my biological parents were. I will forever be grateful to her for that and only wish we had more time together to grow our friendship to the level as many of you had. I already miss her so much."

As she spoke, she watched her mother. Her mother dabbed at her tears when she spoke of having a connection with Alexandria and the tragedies they both endured. And she covered her mouth with the tips of her fingers when she mentioned Alexandria helped her find out who her biological parents were. Her mother looked at her husband and her husband looked at her and you could see her start to sob.

When she finished speaking, Jessica sat down, and Timothy wrapped his arm around her. He pulled her close, and she rested her head on his shoulder. She was exhausted, mentally and physically. Her mother seemed to have remorse for giving her up for adoption. At least, that was how Jessica took her reaction to her words. She was patiently waiting for the funeral to be over. She was hoping to talk to her mother and then take a nap.

Finally, it appeared everyone who wanted to speak had spoken, and the minister asked if there was anyone else that wanted to say something. It dismayed Jessica when she saw her mother's husband walking up to the podium. He was wearing sunglasses and a black suit.

"Good morning everyone, some of you know me as Mathew Brockton. No relation to Arthur there. You know me as a business associate or friend of Richard Gardiner. Today, though, you will all know the truth about who I really am. Out of love and loyalty to my dear cousin Alexandria. I hope someday when we meet again in heaven she will forgive me for my sins and for staying away so long."

As he ended his last sentence, the man at the podium removed his sunglasses and his jet-black hair wig. Revealing the piercing icy blue eyes and strawberry blonde hair of Richard Gardiner. He stood there alive and well, to the dismay of everyone in attendance.

Mary screamed and then fainted. Jimmy rushed to attend to his mother as Arthur rushed up to Richard and ushered him into the manor house. Jessica sat there, stunned. Her father, whom she just found out was biologically hers, who was supposed to be dead, was really alive. She felt a little faint herself.

Jimmy helped Mary to the manor house while the minister gained control of the attendees. The funeral proceeded, and they placed the casket in a horse-drawn carriage to make the small journey to the family cemetery. The mourners walked behind the carriage.

Mary and Jimmy returned to place flowers on the casket. Arthur also returned and placed two dozen red roses on the casket. Jessica couldn't see her mother or father through the crowd of mourners. The minister closed the funeral by inviting all the attendees to join for a lunch on the west lawn.

As attendees mingled and ate, there was definitely a buzz about the return of Richard. Jessica could not find him anywhere, though. She also could not find her mother or her siblings. She finally found Arthur and cornered him.

"Where are they, Arthur? Where is my family?"

"They are safe. I asked them to stay away until everyone leaves the island. You will get to be with them later. Be patient Jessica, this throws a lot of legal issues into the situation and the estate of Alexandria's. And we still don't know who pushed Alexandria down those stairs. Or may I add, who tried to drown you? Your father told me a story about how he survived that tragic sailing accident. If true, there are some legal ramifications there too. It's extremely complicated."

Jessica couldn't process any of what Arthur was saying. *Legal ramifications? How did her father survive? Why did he choose to pretend to be dead all these years?* She found Timothy and told him she needed to go rest. They went to their room in the manor house and tried to rest.

By 3 o'clock in the afternoon, all the mainland attendees were off the island and Arthur had told the inhabitants that the reading of Alexandria's will would have to be postponed. The return of Richard brought so much unease and uncertainty to all involved. Mary was on the verge of a nervous breakdown. *How could he have survived and Benjamin didn't?* That wasn't how it was supposed to happen.

Benjamin was supposed to survive. He was supposed to take the lifeboat and meet her at the beach. They were going to watch the sailboat burn together. However, something had gone horribly wrong and as she sat on the beach that night, she saw the boat and her dreams with Benjamin go up in flames. Benjamin never showed up at the beach. She checked daily for weeks and he never showed. If Richard survived, he had to have known their plan. If he knew, Mary was in serious trouble. She had to figure out what to do.

CHAPTER TWENTY-TWO

His story

WHEN IT WAS DINNER time, Jessica and Timothy made their way down to the dining room. They were stunned to see Richard, Mira, and their three children sitting at the table along with Arthur and an uncomfortable-looking Mary. Jimmy was also sitting at the table. Arthur looked up as Jessica and Timothy took their seats at the table and addressed everyone.

"Now that everyone is here that needs to be here, I would like you, Richard, to tell us all your story."

"Thank you, Arthur. First, I need to address Jessica. I am so sorry your mother and I had to stop all contact with you. Until the sailing accident, we had made it a regular occurrence to spend time with the Greenhalls in order to spend time with you. We couldn't risk your life being endangered if anyone found out I was still alive. The sailboat fire was no accident. They planned it to kill me."

As Richard said that last sentence, he looked straight at Mary and continued with his story.

"My first wife, Mary, was not happy that I was divorcing her, conspired with her lover, Benjamin Timmons, to take me out for a sailing trip and set fire to the boat to cause an explosion killing me. I overheard their plan and made a counter-escape plan with Mira. The only wrinkle was that Alexandria's husband and children went with us, even though I had created a disagreement with her to persuade her not to go. I couldn't back out of the trip. Mary and Benjamin would know something was up. I only wish I could have saved them along with myself. They were the reason I could never face Alexandria with the truth and why I went into hiding as Mathew Brockton."

Jimmy sat listening to Richard's story and watched his biological mother, Mary, intently. Her body language told him everything he needed to know. Richard was telling the truth. She was an accessory to murder. And his biological father was a murderer. Unfortunately, there was no evidence of the allegations Richard was making. There were even no bodies found. Mary was a bundle of nerves that finally exploded.

"Never! I don't know what you are talking about! Yes, I was angry about the divorce and you accusing me of having an affair. The hypocrisy of that is sitting right before us."

She pointed at Jessica.

"To accuse me of conspiring to murder you is ridiculous!"

"I know at this point in time, I have no proof. It is my word against yours. So I am proposing this, in good faith. Sign the divorce papers, finalize the divorce so I am not a polygamist and I will allow you to continue to live on the island as Alexandria had agreed. My life is in Massachusetts now."

Mary knew he was right. There was no proof of the attempted murder of him and the actual murder of his family members. There was proof, though, sitting at the table with them, they both had been unfaithful in their marriage. She could still save face with the divorce since Richard had been MIA since the accident. Most importantly, she could still live in the manor house and keep her status on the island. She agreed to sign the divorce papers and complete the divorce after twenty-three years.

Jimmy was fuming. He was angry to know that there was nothing he could do to prove or disprove his biological parents had murdered four innocent people. He couldn't even stand sitting next to his mother and he didn't know how he felt about her still living on the island. *Was she the one that pushed Alexandria? Was she the one that attempted to drown Jessica?* He couldn't hold in his emotions any longer. He stood up briskly, knocking his chair over, leaned on the table and directed his comments at Arthur.

"Wait! Don't Jessica and I have a say in who lives on the island and who doesn't as heirs to Alexandria's estate? What if we don't want Mary living here?"

Jimmy's outburst shocked everyone. Especially Mary, who burst into tears that her son would not want her on the island. Jessica was still processing the fact her biological parents were sitting at the same table as her. She realized Jimmy had a point. It was their island, too. They had a say. Richard looked at Jimmy perplexed

"Who may I ask are you and why would you inherit Alexandria's estate? Jessica, I understand. And yes, I should have asked your opinion on the matter. I apologize."

As he finished, he looked directly at Jessica.

"Who am I? Well. Let me enlighten you. My name is James Driscoll. Stella and John Driscoll adopted me twenty-five years ago. Until last week, I never knew, or cared, to know who my biological parents were. Alexandria suspected who they were since she orchestrated the adoption. She had done research and orchestrated the three infants born on the same day twenty-five years ago to be reunited. We were all adopted through private closed adoptions through the same law firm. She then had us all tested to prove two of us were of Gardiner lineage. Jessica and I both have Gardiner blood. Jessica through you, Richard, and I through your half-brother, Benjamin Timmons, who fathered me with your wife, Mary. So, Uncle Richard, the decision is not solely yours to make. And until we know who killed Alexandria, I am not making any promises to anyone."

As he finished speaking, he looked at his biological mother and walked out of the room.

Richard sat there, stunned. He knew of the child Mary bore with Benjamin. He also knew of the adoption. They still had the copy of the adoption paperwork that Mira had copied as a file clerk. What he didn't know was Benjamin was his half-brother. This was new information that he had to process. His father had been unfaithful to his mother, just as he had been to Mary. Then the last sentence Jimmy uttered hit him like a ton of bricks. They killed Alexandria. The obituary never mentioned that.

Mary, still crying, now uncontrollably, ran out of the room and they heard her running up the stairs, presumably to her room. Jessica felt bad for her to some extent. She was still numb about her parents, though. Her siblings, who were sitting there through all this, seemed dazed and confused by all that was being discussed. It felt like they were living in some strange twilight zone. Timothy also seemed a little dazed and confused, although he never let go of Jessica's hand the entire time. He was lending her silent support through it all.

Richard slowly overcame his shock.

"Is what he said true? Was Alexandria murdered? And was Benjamin really my half brother?"

"Yes, Alexandria claimed someone pushed her down the stairs. We have found no evidence linking who might have done it. And now that she is dead, all we have is her initial statement. And yes, Alexandria knew Benjamin was your brother and that he was the father of Mary's child. I find it interesting that you didn't specifically ask about whether Jimmy was really Mary and Benjamin's son. Why is that?"

"Arthur, I didn't ask if that was true because I knew that part years ago. Mira worked in the law office that handled the adoptions. She saw the files and told me. She knows what she did, as a minor, was wrong. We never used the information, except to start a friendship with the Greenhalls getting close to our daughter Jessica. Even if we couldn't be her parents, we wanted to watch her grow up. We planned on approaching the Greenhalls when she turned eighteen to see if they would allow us to tell her we were her biological parents. And then the sailboat accident happened and things had to change."

"Well, Richard, your nephew is correct, though. You are not the sole owner of the island. Jimmy and Jessica are the sole heirs named in Alexandria's most recent will. Technically, since you are still alive, your will is void, so you still own your share of the island. I am going to leave you for now because you all have a lot of catching up to do with your daughter. Jessica, I formally introduce you to your father, Richard Gardiner, your mother Mira, your brother Richard, your sister Samantha, and your brother David. Gardiners, meet Jessica, your daughter and sister."

"Thank you, Arthur. We will discuss the legal matters later. I do want to get to know my daughter."

Jessica looked at Arthur as he got up and mouthed the words, "thank you".

The butterflies in her stomach were returning. She didn't know what to say or do. After what seemed like forever, Richard and Mira both got up and walked over to Jessica. They bent over and tried to hug her, which just seemed awkward all around. So Jessica got up out of her chair and hugged them both. Tears streamed down her face. Samantha was the first of the siblings to get up and hug Jessica, too. She started crying.

"I always wanted a sister."

The next sibling to get up was David. He came over and gave Jessica a big bear hug.

"Welcome to the family, sis. So how did you get so good at photography? And how do you like being famous?"

Her brother Richard still seemed a bit unnerved by the whole situation and begrudgingly got up and gave her a hug. He then locked eyes with Timothy.

"So who the hell are you, and where do you fit into this whole crazy situation?"

"Me? Well, I guess you might say I am your sister's boyfriend. At least I think that's where our relationship is heading. My name is Timothy Sullivan. I am a writer for National Geographic magazine. They assigned me to write an article about the ospreys on the island and I requested your sister take the pictures. That's how we met two weeks ago, and it's been a whirlwind since that first day."

"Hey, just because you are my brother doesn't mean you can shake down and interrogate my boyfriend."

Jessica chided, as she nudged her brother Richard with her elbow.

"That's what brothers do."

Responded Richard and David simultaneously, then laughing.

They had broken the ice. They spent the rest of the evening getting to know each other better as a family. When it was time for everyone to go to sleep, Samantha begged Jessica to have a slumber party in her bedroom with her. Jessica obliged and went to Samantha's room. The one she had been told she could stay in for the evening. Timothy jokingly teased Jessica he would be lonely without her and she kissed him goodnight and said he would be fine.

Timothy was nervous not having Jessica by his side in this house. He was worried about her safety. The allegations brought against Mary by Jessica's father didn't sit well with him. He replayed the evening that they almost drowned Jessica in his mind. *Could Mary have been the one to try the drowning? She had plenty of motives. She also had the motive to kill Alexandria.*

CHAPTER TWENTY-THREE

Confessions

MARY LOCKED HERSELF IN her room and threw herself on her bed. She was heartbroken. The way Jimmy now looked at her with disgust and contempt was unbearable. She had to think of a way to get back in his favor. She didn't know how she was going to do it, though. He had worked security on the island since he was eighteen. He took his job seriously and believed in law, order, and justice.

She opened a bottle of wine from her private stash and poured herself a glass. When she had drank half of it, her nerves had settled a bit and she felt calmer. She had to think rationally. Her home and lifestyle depended on it.

It was generous of Richard to offer her to stay on the island in exchange for the divorce. She only wished she had known that Benjamin was Richard's half-brother when he was alive. If they had known that, things could have been different. Why had Alexandria kept that a secret all these years? *Damn bitch, had messed up so much of her life*. Making her give up her only child for adoption.

As she finished her first glass of wine and poured herself another one, she thought taking a relaxing bath would help her think. She placed the bottle of wine and her full glass on a chair next to her tub. She turned the water on and let the tub fill. Her cell phone rang in her bedroom and she went to answer it. There was no one on the other end, so she hung up. She went to go back to the tub, and it rang again, so again she answered it and no one was there. Annoyed, she turned off her phone and went back to the tub.

She drank more of her wine and undressed. Stepping into the tub, she wobbled slightly, feeling off balance. As she slid herself into the tub, the warmth of the water enveloped her. Relaxing more and more, she finished her second glass of wine and poured herself a third. After a few sips, she felt drowsy, and she closed her eyes.

Soon she was dreaming of her and Benjamin and the life they had wanted together. The dream morphed. In the dream, she was on the beach. Jimmy was sitting next to her, and she was trying to explain to him why his father and she had planned to kill Richard. Alexandria's family was just collateral damage. She had felt guilty about that for the last twenty-three years. She had lost Benjamin, too. Wasn't that enough punishment?

In the dream, she pleaded with Jimmy to forgive her and to understand. He was angry and refused to forgive her. He accused her of trying to drown Jessica and of killing Alexandria. She denied having anything to do with those instances, however; he refused to believe her. He told her he was going to go to the police. She couldn't bear the heartbreak and she couldn't bear him telling the police.

She picked up a rock next to her and hit him in the head with it. As he slumped over, she kept repeating.

"I am not a murderer!"

Then everything went dark.

In the morning Stella was quietly making breakfast for the houseful of inhabitants. Jimmy had filled her in on what had transpired the night before. It still disgusted him with the knowledge his mother had conspired to kill people. All for prestige and money. He hated the thought of becoming like that.

One by one the Gardiners awoke and came down for breakfast. They were all very polite and appreciative of the home cooked breakfast and coffee. Jessica and Samantha came down together, giggling like schoolgirls. Shortly after, Arthur and Timothy emerged from their rooms to dine with the rest of them.

The only inhabitant that did not come down for breakfast was Mary. Stella sent Betty to go check on her. And within minutes, they could hear blood-curdling screams from Betty throughout the house. Chaos erupted as everyone went running to find out what brought on the screaming.

To everyone's horror, they found Mary dead in her bathtub. On the chair next to the tub was an empty wineglass, an empty bottle of wine, an empty pill bottle, and a note written by Mary to Jimmy.

My Dear son Jimmy,

I am sorry I am a murderer. I love you with all my heart and always have. The thought of you hating me is one that I can not bear. I would rather be dead than see the disgust and contempt for me in your eyes anymore. I helped to conspire to kill my husband, Richard. Benjamin was not supposed to die. We were supposed to live happily ever after on the island together. Instead, I lived a lonely existence for the last twenty-three years. Alexandria's family was not part of the plan. Unfortunately, they became collateral damage. I tried to drown Jessica the first night she was here. I also tampered with the throttle on her ATV. And yes, I pushed Alexandria down the stairs.

Someday I hope you will forgive me and understand. I will always love you.

Love your MOM.

Jimmy read the note with tears in his eyes. Then he called the State Police.

Richard and Mira sat with everyone in the parlor. Their first questions surrounded the confession about Jessica almost being drowned and the ATV throttle. It mortified them their daughter was the target of a psychopathic murderer. The police came and the coroner came.

The police interviewed everyone in the house. With the note, the empty wineglass, the empty pill bottle, and the empty bottle of wine and no evidence of the contrary, the police ruled Mary's death a suicide and entered her note into evidence in Alexandria's case. With her confession, they were going to close the case. They also closed the investigation into the incidents with Jessica.

The mood in the house was a somber one and for the second time in two weeks, they planned a funeral on the island. Jessica didn't want to stay on the island. She used the excuse that she and Timothy had already booked the room at the bed-and-breakfast. She couldn't shake the feeling that something was off about Mary's death, but she couldn't put her finger on it.

She needed to get off the island. Her parents understood. They were feeling creeped out about staying in a house that someone had just died in and they stayed at Lena and Steve's until they could have Mary's funeral.

They all hugged Jimmy and Arthur and told them if they needed anything to call them and headed for the mainland. The revelations still shook Jimmy in the note and the death of his biological mom.

At the bed-and-breakfast, Jessica could finally express her feelings to Timothy about Mary's death.

"None of it makes sense. How could she have been the one to drown me? She would have been wet, right? There wasn't enough time for her to go through the passage and change clothes before entering the room, was there? I feel like that night is becoming a blur. So many revelations in such a short time. I can't even think straight."

"I don't know, Jessica. It seemed like an eternity to me when I was trying to get inside the bathroom. She confessed, though. Jimmy and others verified it was her handwriting. Why would she confess to something she didn't do and then commit suicide?"

"Something just doesn't seem right. I don't know why, but something seems off about it, that's all. I think I just need some sleep."

They both agreed a good night's sleep away from the island and the manor house would be beneficial to them. Jessica filled Timothy in on her slumber party with her sister and how she actually had fun. She fell asleep telling him how happy she was that she finally had found her biological family and she would do everything in her power to help him find his.

Timothy wasn't sure he wanted to know about his biological family anymore. Seeing everything Jessica had been through in the last two weeks, he couldn't imagine having to go through it all himself. Plus, he was content with starting his own family with Jessica. He didn't need anyone else.

After breakfast the next morning, Jessica and Timothy met Lena and Steve. Lena apologized to Jessica for watching her and whispering about her in the café when she and her mother first saw her. She explained she just couldn't get over how much she looked like her mom.

Rita stopped by and was visibly upset about her cousin Mary's death. Lena filled in Jessica about the relationship between her mother and Mary. She also found out about Rita having Lena at a young age. Lena quietly whispered to Jessica. She wished she knew who her biological father was. However, her mother was always tight-lipped about that.

They all did some shopping at the outlets in Riverhead. While they were there, Timothy and Jessica snuck away to his house for a bit. Jessica found it spotless in his bachelor pad. It was small, but quaint. It seemed to work for him, considering he traveled a lot for his different writing assignments. He had a small yard, and the house was a two-bedroom ranch. After a brief discussion, Jessica convinced Timothy that they should just stay at his house until Mary's funeral in two days.

When they told the others they wouldn't be returning to East Hampton until the funeral, there was a disappointment by Richard and Mira. However, they remembered young love and the desire to shut the rest of the world out. They said their goodbyes, and they told each other they'd see each other in a few days.

The further Jessica got away from the island, the more relaxed she felt. Timothy cooked a nice romantic dinner and even lit candles on his table. They settled in on the couch after dinner and watched a movie. Jessica felt so at ease with him. She couldn't believe they had only met two weeks ago.

Timothy's phone ringing interrupted their solitude. It wound up being his editor telling him about an assignment he was being sent on in the everglades of Florida to do an article on the snake overpopulation. He tried requesting Jessica be his photographer again, but his editor stated they already had a photographer lined up. He would leave the day after Mary's funeral.

Jessica was okay with not going, considering the snakes petrified her. Oddly, she received a phone call from her agent about an assignment for her to photograph the Cliffs of Moher in Ireland. She needed to leave the day after Mary's funeral as well. Sadness overwhelmed her, and she cried. She knew she needed to work and Timothy did, too. The thought of being so far away from him even for a few days, though, really was difficult to work through. This would be the first test of their relationship and their careers.

Knowing it would be one of the last nights in a while they would be together, they spent the night making love to one another.

In two days, they made the drive back out to East Hampton and back to the island for Mary's funeral. It wasn't as big or as well attended as Alexandria's had been, but it was big enough. There was still buzzing about the return of Richard. News had spread fast about Mary's suicide and that she had confessed to the attempted murder of her husband. Knowing that helped people to understand why Richard had gone into hiding under a different alias.

When Jessica told Arthur that she would leave the country the next day, it flustered him. They still needed to go over Alexandria's will and get her estate straightened out. They decided that they would have to read the will after everyone left Mary's funeral.

CHAPTER TWENTY-FOUR

The will

BEFORE THE READING OF the will, Arthur, Richard, Jimmy, and Jessica sat down to discuss the logistics of how they were going to work together to manage the island. With Mary being deceased, that meant the manor house was empty. Jessica had no desire to live on the island or in the manor house. She felt Jimmy should be the one to live there since he had the most connection to the island.

Richard agreed. His life was in Massachusetts with his family. He felt confident Jimmy could run things on the island and also felt he should live in the manor house. Richard would remove any of his belongings, if any remained. He assumed, though, that Mary had gotten rid of them years ago.

Jimmy was agreeable to running the island. He just wasn't sure how he felt about living in the manor house. His mind was still processing all that had transpired over the last two weeks. Finding out who his biological mom was and losing her in a week's time was overwhelming. Not to mention finding out both his biological parents were murderers. It made him question whether he had any psychopathic tendencies. He could not share those thoughts with anyone for fear of others thinking he was dangerous or incompetent. He agreed to at least try living in the house for a period.

There were still things that made Jessica nervous about telling the island inhabitants who Alexandria's heirs were. Mary's suicide still didn't sit right with her. Neither did her confessions. It did not convince her they were safe.

"Arthur, is there any way we can keep our lineage to Alexandria a secret? Or at least Jimmy's?"

"I suppose we could, but why should we?"

"To be honest, there are things about Mary's death that don't sit right with me. I can't pinpoint what exactly it is. I just don't feel that we are safe."

"Jimmy, what are your thoughts?"

Jimmy was listening to the conversation between Arthur and Jessica. He thought he was the only one that questioned Mary's death. Hearing Jessica's concerns made him feel a little less crazy.

"I agree with Jessica. I can't pinpoint what isn't settling right with Mary's death, either. However, I do not feel as if we are safe. I feel Jessica and Richard are safer being away from the island. So I agree, not telling everyone that I am actually a Gardiner is the safest bet."

They all agreed they would not disclose the lineage of Jimmy. Jimmy left the meeting to tell everyone it was time for the reading of the will. The others joined the rest of Richard's family and Timothy and explained to them quickly what they were going to do.

Once everyone came together, Arthur addressed the group.

"Good evening all, thank you for being patient and waiting for Alexandria's will to be read. I am going to ask you all to remain quiet while I read the will and explain things. When I am done, you can ask questions you may have."

He then cleared his throat and continued.

"The last will and testament of Alexandria Cromwell. The declarations state: This is my will. All previous wills and codicils are void. I live in Manhattan, New York. I am widowed. Nomination of executor: I nominate the individual or bank, or trust company below as the first choice as executor to carry out the instructions of this will. No bond or other security of any kind will be required of any party acting in a fiduciary capacity for my estate/ or any trust created through my will. I grant to my executor the following powers. The power to exercise all powers of an absolute owner of property. Power to keep, sell at public or private sale, exchange, grant options on, invest and reinvest, and otherwise deal with real or personal property. The power to borrow money and pledge any property to secure loans along with the power to divide and distribute property in cash or in kind. The power to compromise and release claims with or without considerations. Power to pay my legally enforceable debts, funeral expenses, expenses of last illness, and all expenses in connection with the administration of my estate and the trusts created by my will. The power to employ attorneys, accountants and other persons for services and advice and any other powers conferred upon executors wherever my executor may act. If the first choice does not serve, then I nominate the second choice to serve. My first choice is Arthur Brockton, my personal attorney. My second choice is Allison Simmons, my friend and CEO of Cromwell Real Estate Investments. The disposition of property. Specific gifts of cash. I make the following cash gift (s) to the following person (s) or organization (s) named below. I initial my name in the box next to each gift. To Stella and John Driscoll, I leave $100,000. If Stella and John Driscoll do not survive me, I leave this gift to their heirs-at-law. If they have no heirs-at-law, they shall distribute the gift as residue of my estate."

Arthur continued listing each employee of the island, except for one. He continued reading the will.

"I leave the whole of my company Cromwell Real Estate Investments and Gardiner Island to my heirs at law. I leave in place the agreement with Mary Gardiner as to her living on the island. Residuary Estate. Except for specific gift (s) made above, I leave my residuary estate, after the payment of any estate tax, as follows, and I initial my name in each box after each gift. I leave a third of my residual estate to Arthur Brockton. To Jessica Greenhall, I leave 33.34% of my residual estate. To Jimmy Driscoll, I leave 33.34% of my residual estate. If any beneficiary of this gift does not survive me, I leave his/her share to their heirs-at-law. If there are no heirs-at-law, then their share will be distributed as residue of my estate. General provisions. Severability. If any provisions of this will are deemed unenforceable, then the remaining provisions shall remain in full force and effect.

Survivorship. I shall deem no beneficiary to survive me unless such beneficiary remains alive 30 days after my death. Any beneficiary prohibited by law from inheriting property from me shall be treated as having failed to survive me."

As Arthur finished reading the will, the room was abuzz with conversation among the inhabitants. One inhabitant walked out of the room without saying a word to anyone. The only one that seemed to notice was Jessica. She had been watching the reactions intently of everyone in the room. Everyone seemed pleased except for the one person not mentioned in the will, Samuel.

Jessica approached Arthur and quietly asked him.

"Why wasn't Samuel mentioned in Alexandria's will?"

"Samuel was not and is not an employee of Alexandria. Mary hired him and she paid him. I need to catch up with him and discuss that with him. Jimmy has said that he wants to keep him on and take over paying his salary. Do you agree with that?"

"Yes, I absolutely want to keep him on. I hope Alexandria did not slight him by not gifting him money like the others, though?"

"I will let him know. Mary's lawyer has also already informed me she left him a sizeable gift in her will, so I will inform him of that as well."

"Thank you, Arthur, I must be saying my goodbyes for now. I have to get home and pack for my assignment in Ireland. I leave tomorrow."

Timothy and Jessica said their goodbyes and headed back to Jessica's house in Connecticut. They both would catch flights to their respective assignments the next day. Jessica was forlorn that she did not have more time to spend with her family, however, she felt hopeful that when she returned, they could get together.

The inhabitants seemed happy with the fact they left Jimmy in charge of the island. They explained that both Richard and Jessica, the only known heirs-at-law of Alexandria, had requested that Jimmy would be in charge of the island. It was also explained that Jessica had asked Alexandria to name Jimmy as a residuary recipient to compensate him for his work of running things on the island. Everyone seemed pleased with this explanation. All the inhabitants went to their homes, content that their jobs and homes were secure.

Richard and his family headed home to Massachusetts. Richard and Mira felt freer knowing the truth was finally out there about them. Their adult children were in shock at the events that had transpired over the last several days. They were happy though that they got to meet their big sister. Even Richard Jr. had warmed up to her.

Arthur caught up to Samuel and explained why there was no mention of him in Alexandria's will. He also explained Mary's will. Samuel seemed surprised that it named him in Mary's and Arthur seemed to think it made up for not being named in Alexandria's. The two men parted ways and went about their own duties.

The silence in the manor house was deafening to Jimmy, who, after everyone had left, was alone. He worried he might go insane being all alone with his thoughts in the big house. *Is that what happened to Mary?* Thinking about his biological mother lead to him remembering the conversation with Jessica earlier. He went up to Mary's room to look around.

Shivers ran down his spine when Jimmy walked into Mary's room. They had left everything the way they found it that fateful morning. When he went into the bathroom, he remembered what he had missed in the bathroom during the investigation into Jessica's near drowning. Opening the linen closet, he found that there indeed was another secret passageway leading up to the attic. There were passageways from every bathroom to the attic. He wasn't sure what the original purpose was, however; he knew they made it easy for someone to sneak around the house undetected.

The question in his mind, though, was, could Mary have attempted to drown Jessica, sneak back to her room, change clothes, and then reappear with no one noticing? He was determined to test the theory and gathered the items needed to simulate the situation. He attempted to submerge a makeshift dummy, escape, change clothes in Mary's room, and then reappear as if nothing had been done. The first attempt was an utter failure. After locking the door and turning off the lights, it was nearly impossible to move around the bathroom purposefully. She would have had to have had night vision goggles.

Every member of the security team, including himself, had a pair, so borrowing or finding a pair was not impossible. He used his pair for the next attempt at recreating the scenario. No matter how many times he attempted the scenario, he could not escape, change out of the wet clothes, and reappear in less than 20 minutes. Far longer than it took for Mary to appear that night from what Timothy and Jessica had stated.

According to this information, Mary could not have been the one to attempt drowning Jessica. Even though she confessed to doing so in her suicide note. If Mary didn't do it, then maybe she didn't actually commit suicide. How would Jimmy prove that, though? He would discretely keep digging and investigating everything that occurred in the last two weeks. If Mary was not the murderer, then he or she was still walking amongst them.

He had to be very careful with who he trusted any information with as well.

   For now, he decided not to tell anyone else.

CHAPTER TWENTY-FIVE
Family Thanksgiving

WEEKS WENT BY AND Timothy and Jessica moved in together. Jessica precipitated the decision coming home from her Ireland assignment to find her house broken into and ransacked. They took nothing of value, although the one thing that was taken Jessica hadn't told the police, her family, or even Timothy.

Things had been so quiet since Mary's death that she didn't want to upset anyone. She didn't even know the significance of the stolen item. It was the note she had received prior to going back to Gardiners Island for Alexandria's funeral. Nothing had happened to her when she returned to the island, so she felt it had been one of her many crazed stalker-type fans.

Still, the break-in made her feel vulnerable and unsettled and that helped push Timothy into the decision to move in with her. Timothy put his house on the market and moved in with Jessica.

Jessica made a weekly trip to Manhattan to sit in on the board meeting of the Cromwell Real Estate Investment Corporation. She was grateful for the CEO, Allison. Alexandria knew how to hire the right people to get the job done.

Allison was intelligent, resourceful, and was always full of innovative ideas. Jessica admired her and felt very confident in her running the company. Richard also attended the weekly board meetings, along with Jimmy.

Afterward, the three would meet to discuss the island and how things were going there. Jimmy was managing things there well and still hadn't told the others he had figured out about Mary's death and confession not being plausible. He was still doing information gathering.

A week before Thanksgiving, Jimmy invited the family to the manor house to have a traditional Thanksgiving dinner. They were all planning on attending and all were going to stay at the house. Jimmy had told everyone that for safety and security reasons, he had installed a padlock on the kitchen door to the attic and he was the only person with a key as an added measure.

The night before Thanksgiving, they all returned to the island. Stella was busy preparing some of the dinner dishes and baking several pies. The aromas made everyone's mouths water with the anticipation of the next day's feast. If anyone dared enter the kitchen though to steal a taste, she met them with a tap of a wooden spoon to their hands.

Jimmy had converted the parlor into a den. It had a pool table and a ping-pong table in it. He replaced the antique sofa and other furniture with more modern comfortable couches and chairs. The family approved, and they all enjoyed challenging each other to both games.

The next morning, Stella cooked up a grand breakfast to start the morning festivities. She made all the different pancakes, eggs, bacon, and sausages. The entire family enjoyed every morsel.

Jessica had never had a big family. She also never had a big traditional Thanksgiving. While it was all new experiences for her, she was soaking up all the fabulous memories they were all making.

Mira was content knowing all her children were finally all together with her and Richard. She watched as her children bonded with their older sister more with each passing day. There were so many blessings to be thankful for this Thanksgiving. She knew she would etch this in her memory as her favorite holiday memory.

When they all sat down to dinner, they said a blessing, shared what they were each thankful for, and then ate. Richard was happily sitting at the head of the table. He was glad to be with his family, however, he still had pangs of guilt and sadness regarding Alexandria and her family. He missed them all.

Sitting at the table he had grown up at brought back all those bittersweet memories. This is what he had always wanted for himself, though. A family of his own, sitting enjoying a holiday meal together. He knew soon the family would expand as his children settled down. As he looked at his son Richard with his girlfriend Danielle sitting next to him and Jessica with Timothy sitting next to her. He wondered which couple would get married first.

Danielle and Richard had known each other for years and just recently became a couple. Timothy and Jessica had only met months ago and had dove headfirst into their relationship. He couldn't judge either couple. He had done the slow and steady with Mary and the fast and furious with Mira. All he wanted for his children was for them to be happy and healthy.

After dinner, the family retired back into the den. They had a ping-pong tournament going, that was getting pretty competitive. Jimmy was currently in the lead. He was glad everyone was enjoying themselves. He also felt confident in all his security measures. There had been no strange accidents or deaths in the month following Mary's apparent suicide and confession. It was good to see everyone relaxed and having fun.

Timothy and Richard had left the room briefly and, on their return, were both smiling wryly. Jessica was playing a fierce game of ping-pong against her sister Samantha, in which she was narrowly winning. When she had won, Timothy approached her, grabbed her arm and raised it in the air, proclaiming her a winner. As he dropped her arm, he dropped to one knee and continued holding her hand.

"Jessica, it's been a whirlwind ride for the last several weeks, but there is no one else I would rather spend the rest of my life with. Will you marry me?"

"Yes!"

The entire room erupted with excitement and congratulations. Mira had tears of joy. Richard proudly smiled and slapped Timothy on the back in congratulations. Samantha couldn't wait to help her sister plan her wedding. David and

Richard Jr. welcomed Timothy as their brother-in-law to be. Jimmy congratulated the couple and offered for them to hold the wedding on the island if they wished.

Emotions overjoyed Jessica. A few months earlier, she hadn't even known who she was. She had no family that she knew of and, by a weird twist of fate, she had found them. She also had found the love of her life. Something a few short months ago she had not even thought possible.

Nothing could take the smile off her face. The rest of the weekend, the family helped Jimmy decorate the manor house for Christmas. They even went to a local Christmas tree farm and cut the biggest tree they could find.

As they decorated the tree, they made plans to spend the Christmas holiday together at the manor house. They also discussed possible wedding dates. Jessica and Timothy decided on a July wedding. They thought having the wedding in the manor gardens would be simply wonderful, as they forgot all about their first few times on the island and the bad luck that had befallen them.

Soon, it was time for them all to leave and head home. The family thanked Jimmy for his hospitality and said their goodbyes to each other. They all left the island with hope in their hearts that the tragedies of the island's past were all behind them. Jimmy breathed a sigh of relief as they all drove away to the rickety ferry that he had kept them all safe this time.

There were no signs of trouble the whole long weekend. He had the security team on constant patrols. No one had reported seeing anyone or anything out of the ordinary. He thought Mary had been the intended target all along. That all the other accidents and near-death experiences were to frame Mary. Jimmy couldn't think of a motive, though.

Mary had left everything to the one employee she had hired on the island, Samuel. He wasn't aware he even stood to inherit anything until after her death. That meant inheritance could not be a motive. Samuel had been angry at first with not receiving anything from Alexandria's estate, but then learning he had inherited everything from

Mary, made up for it. Mary had always treated him well, and he was grateful for that.

Mary's death nagged at Jimmy. He knew he was missing something, but he couldn't figure out what. Every day, he made his usual rounds on the island. He would stop at the beach she frequently sat at, waiting for his father to return after the fateful boating accident. He still couldn't believe they had conspired to kill Richard. It made him mad his parents were capable of such atrocities. He was madder with himself for caring about who killed his mother, but he told himself it was his job to know and keep everyone safe.

That's what he would focus on now, keeping everyone who stepped foot on the island safe. As he did his evening rounds, he looked at the rickety old ferry and decided at their next meeting he would suggest replacing it. He knew Jessica would probably agree since she always complained about how it made her nervous.

He would talk to Captain Bill, who drove the ferry, and get his recommendations. Jimmy felt they should do it before Jessica and Timothy's wedding. He wanted his cousin's day to be just perfect. They had grown quite fond of each other over the last few months, despite their rocky start.

Jessica and Timothy got home, and they sat together on their couch, looking at wedding websites on Jessica's laptop. She couldn't believe they were planning their wedding. She didn't want it to be too fancy, although with it being on the island, she knew there would be a slight air of fanciness. Her sister and her mother were already texting her all kinds of wedding ideas. She felt grateful she could share her excitement with them. She also knew that Timothy had no family to share his excitement with.

Jessica was even more determined now to find his family. She encouraged him to log in to the genealogy website he had submitted his DNA to months ago. When his results had first come in over a month ago, there were several hundred distant cousins and some 4th cousins. However, there had been no closer relatives. This time, when he logged in, there was a match with a second cousin. He messaged the person to find out as much information from them about their family as he could. And then came the waiting game for a response.

Timothy didn't know what he would do with the information, since he did not know what part of this family's tree would be a help to him. He made a promise to Jessica to check his messages daily and his matches. Together, they were determined to find out who he was.

CHAPTER TWENTY-SIX

In the shadows

WHEN THEY HEARD THE family was coming to the island for Thanksgiving, they grumbled. There wasn't enough time to really plan any proper welcoming. The anger was brewing and there was no release.

Finding the padlock on the kitchen door to the attic increased their anger. Why was it padlocked? *Damn it, Jimmy. You and your high horse security measures*. They mumbled to themselves. They would have to resort to spying on the family from the outside of the house this time. Until they could figure out a more sophisticated way to hear what was going on.

As the family arrived on the island, the hatred for them all simmered. Revenge would be sweet, eventually. They would bide their time and plan carefully. Calculating every move they made. Everything that was to occur had to be planned just right.

Watching the family the first night was nauseating. Their laughter carried away from the house as they watched from the shadows of the gardens. It was tempting to ruin their fun with a few scare tactics. Patience was not their strong suit, however, they resisted.

The worst was watching through the windows as they decorated the Christmas tree. That reminded them of their childhood and the Christmas mornings they endured. That was if their mother even was sober enough to realize what the date was. Or if she wasn't busy entertaining one of her gentlemen friends.

After the family left for the weekend, they had heard rumors they would be back for the Christmas holiday. That gave them time to do some planning. Not much time, however, enough to do some prep work. They also heard about the wedding in July. No actual date, though. That was disappointing. They secretly hoped for the fourth of July.

That would be poetic justice. They smiled and laughed at the thought. Fireworks and explosions would make a perfect distraction. Rubbing their hands together with anticipatory excitement, they started making plans.

This will be an epic ending for them and a beautiful new beginning for me.

About Author

A former paraeducator, novice genealogist, turned author D.M. Foley is an award-winning author. The first edition of this book received The New York Best Sellers Gold Award in December 2021. She lives in Southeastern, Ct, with her husband, three sons, and her mom.

You can follow her on her social media accounts at:

D.M. Foley - Author Page on Facebook

@d.m._foley on Instagram and TikTok

@DMFoley author on Twitter

Contact information:

d.m.foleyauthor@gmail.com

D.M. Foley

D.M. FOLEY

54 Main Street

P.O. Box 735

Jewett City, CT

06351

If you would like a signed bookplate, send a self-addressed stamped envelope to the above address.

Books In This Trilogy

Family Ties The Lyons Garden Book One
Erasing Secrets The Lyons Garden Book Two
Pawns The Lyons Garden Book Three

Books By This Author

Family Ties The Lyons Garden Book One
Erasing Secrets The Lyons Garden Book Two
Pawns The Lyons Garden Book Three

Deric Dream Changer Book 1 Of The Dream Walkers Series

The Killer Trip (To be released June 2023)